I'll Be
THERE

ANNE SCHRAFF

SADDLEBACK
PUBLISHING

URBAN UNDERGROUND

SADDLEBACK
P U B L I S H I N G
www.sdlback.com

ISBN-13: 978-1-62250-763-4
ISBN-10: 1-62250-763-0
eBook: 978-1-61247-974-3

Printed in Guangzhou, China
NOR/1213/CA21302313

18 17 16 15 14   1 2 3 4 5

CHAPTER ONE

Not everyone at Cesar Chavez High School liked the senior class president, Ernesto Sandoval. Most did, but he had enemies too. Rod Garcia, who wanted to be president of the senior class, bitterly resented that Ernesto was president. Clay Aguirre, a rising football star, hated Ernesto for taking Naomi Martinez away from him in their junior year. Clay had abused Naomi, but he refused to own his role in losing the girl he loved.

There were other seniors who resented that Ernesto was smart and good-looking and so well liked. But Ernesto didn't focus on any of that. He had helped to establish several new programs at Chavez, and he was proud of them: for example, seniors were now mentoring seniors who were having problems academically and/or socially. In another mentoring program, seniors were "adopting" at-risk freshmen.

Ernesto participated in the at-risk mentoring program and had a little "brother" named Richie Loranzo. Richie had no family to care for him because his father shot his mother to death in a horrific domestic abuse incident. Richie lived in foster care, and he desperately needed a friend.

Naomi Martinez was big "sister" to Angel Roma, a girl struggling to help care for a sick grandmother. Abel Ruiz, Ernesto's best friend, had taken Bobby Padilla, a rebellious runaway, under his wing.

Ernesto never asked Richie for details about what it had been like in his house when his parents were together. He thought if the boy ever wanted to open up about it, he'd listen. All Ernesto wanted to do was give the boy some fun experiences, like when the seniors and the freshmen they were mentoring went camping in the mountains.

After school on Friday, Ernesto and Naomi took Richie and Angel over to Naomi's house on Bluebird Street. Naomi's brother Orlando performed with a Latin band in Los Angeles, and lately he'd been getting a lot of attention. Orlando was a handsome young man, and his song "Estrellas fugaces" was a hit. That song was chosen as the theme of the homecoming dance at Chavez High, and Orlando surprised and delighted everyone by making a personal appearance at the dance. The girls went a little crazy.

When Ernesto and Orlando met at the Martinez house, Orlando had a guitar in his arms. He led the way out to the magical little garden Felix Martinez had created in the backyard of the house. Everyone in the neighborhood was amazed that Naomi and Orlando's father, who was a gruff person, could have carved elves and made a rock garden. Orlando sat on the stone bench and began to strum his guitar.

Naomi's mother, Linda Martinez, served cookies and punch to Angel Roma and Richie Loranzo, but soon both freshmen followed the sound of guitar music to the garden. When Angel Roma saw Orlando Martinez, she was amazed. "I've seen your videos on YouTube, and I check out your Facebook page all the time. Are you *really* Orlando Martinez?"

Orlando grinned at the dark-haired four-teen-year-old. "Yeah, I guess I am," he said.

"What are you doing *here*?" Richie Loranzo found the voice to ask. "Why would a famous guy be sitting in the back-yard of a house in the *barrio*?"

"He's my brother, Richie," Naomi said, laughing. "Orlando is my big brother."

"For real?" Richie gasped, his eyes bigger than Ernesto had ever seen them.

"I think so," Naomi said, laughing again. "I know he was always around when I was a little girl, and my parents told me he was my brother, so I guess he is."

"You're really *hot*," Angel said.

"Hey, thanks," Orlando said. Naomi was

4

so used to her brother that she never really noticed how good-looking he was with his thick, curly hair, his marvelous dark eyes, and his brilliant smile. "Would you guys like to hear a song?" Orlando asked.

"Yeah!" Angel said. Richie nodded.

Orlando sang a classic Mexican folk song that brought Felix Martinez, his father, outside.

"Sounds great, Orlando," Mr. Martinez said.

When Orlando finished his song, Naomi said, "Dad, this is Angel Roma, the freshman I am mentoring. And this is Richie Loranzo, Ernie's freshman."

Felix Martinez looked at the freshmen and said, "Hi there, kids," in a half-hearted way. The eyebrow over his left eye went up a little, a sign that all was not right.

Ernesto volunteered to take Angel and Richie home after they had eaten their fill of cookies, but Angel hesitated. "Mr. Martinez," she said to Orlando, "may I have your autograph?"

"Yeah, sure, *muchacha*," Orlando said. "Just call me Orlando. The only Mr. Martinez around here is my dad." Orlando fished out a photo of himself from his wallet and wrote on the back "To *mi amiga* Angel Roma."

"Wow," Angel said. "Thanks!"

"Could I have one too?" Richie asked shyly.

"Sure," Orlando said, and signed the back of the photo "To *mi amigo* Richie Loranzo."

Ernesto had never seen the two freshmen so excited as they followed him to his Volvo. Ernesto would have been happy about how everything went, but he felt uneasy. There was something wrong with the look on Felix Martinez's face. Something was bothering him. Ernesto felt bad about leaving Naomi alone with a brewing storm, so after he dropped the kids at their homes, he circled back to Bluebird Street, just to make sure everything was cool.

It wasn't.

When Ernesto pulled into the driveway of the Martinez house, he heard loud, angry voices. A big argument was underway. Ernesto's suspicions that all was not well were correct.

"Pop," Orlando shouted, "he's just a little kid. He's a fourteen-year-old kid. Why are you blowing a gasket over a poor little *muchacho*?"

"Oh man," Ernesto muttered to himself. He went up the walk and rapped on the door, causing a brief lull in the argument.

"Wonderful," Felix Martinez stormed, "now somebody else is here." When he swung open the door, his face was dark with rage. "Listen, Ernie," he said, "I like you. You're a great kid, but you got yourself and my little girl in one lousy deal playing buddy-buddy to some criminal kids."

"Mr. Martinez," Ernesto said as he came in. "Our at-risk mentoring program is just for seniors to help kids who have challenges. The freshmen aren't criminals."

"Okay, maybe the girl Naomi got stuck

with is okay, I don't know nothin' about that, but this Loranzo kid. You maybe don't know the story there … his old man—" Felix Martinez stormed.

Before Ernesto had a chance to explain that he did know Richie's background, Orlando shouted in a voice as loud and out of control as his father's: "You're making a *bobo* of yourself like usual, Pop. It's not the *muchacho's* fault that his father took out his mom. That's all the more reason Ernie has got to help the kid. Are you *loco*? What should we do, punish the poor kid because of what happened with his parents? Yeah, his father did an awful thing, and he's in prison for it. Hasn't the *muchacho* been punished enough by what went down?"

Linda Martinez stood in the doorway, her face transfixed with sorrow. Naomi went to her father and put her hand on his arm. "Dad, we *know* what happened to Richie's mother. *We know*. The boy was traumatized. He didn't even want to come to school anymore. He lives in a foster home, and he's been a total loner. Now his foster parents told us that since Ernie and the rest of us are helping him, he's actually coming alive again. We're helping him heal. Don't you understand, Dad?" she said.

"Please. He don't understand anything," Orlando bellowed. "He never did."

"Listen to the kid," Felix Martinez growled. "The big shot in LA. He ain't got any respect for his old man. His face is all over the Internet, and he thinks he knows it all."

"Ay!" Orlando yelled, striding across the room. "Mom, Naomi, how about if we go down to Hortencia's for tamales? Let the old grizzly bear stew in his own juice. You too, Ernie, come with us."

"Thanks," Ernesto said. "I think I'll hang around here for a while."

With everybody else gone, Ernesto sat down in one of the overstuffed chairs and said, "Mr. Martinez, I understand how you feel. You hear about a terrible crime and you naturally don't want your kid involved with those people."

Felix Martinez looked at Ernesto and said, "Listen, Ernie, you got a good heart. I know that. I just don't want my little girl mixed up with bad people. That Loranzo guy, the boy's father, he murdered his wife and the kid saw it. It was in all the papers. You were still up in LA then. It was a big deal all over the *barrio*. The poor lady had a big funeral at Our Lady of Guadalupe Church. They wouldn't let the father come 'cause he was in jail."

"I understand, Mr. Martinez," Ernesto said, "but the boy is being raised by good people now. I met his foster parents, and they're decent people. We're all trying to help Richie. He lost his mother. He lost all the years of love and support a mother gives. And he lost his father too. He has suffered so much, and he's a good kid. He cares about people. He'll go out of his way to help Angel Roma, the little girl you met. I think we can help Richie grow up to be a good man in spite of what happened. I think he deserves that. Richie lost his parents, and it's not fair that he should lose the people who are trying to help him now."

Felix Martinez was silent for a moment. He crossed and uncrossed his legs. He looked uncomfortable. "I see where you're coming from, Ernie," he said finally. "Listen, I got nothing against the kid. I'm sorry for him and all that. I mean, I trust you, Ernie. If you know the kid and he don't, you know, have bad tendencies like his old man … I guess it's okay for you and Naomi to hang with him and, you know, help him along. I mean, the kid didn't do anything wrong. I know that."

"Yeah, Mr. Martinez," Ernesto said. "I'm glad you see it that way."

"Sure, Ernie, sure," Felix Martinez said. He even smiled a little.

When Ernesto went out to his Volvo, there was a text message from Naomi on his phone.

"R U OK? ILU," it said.

Ernesto smiled and called Naomi. She was at Hortencia's with her mother and Orlando.

"Everything is cool, babe," Ernesto said. "I got your father to calm down and look at it more reasonably. He's okay with it now."

"Ernie," Naomi said, "you're wonderful."

Ernesto heard Orlando in the background say, "How did he do it? Did he throw a bucket of cold water over his head?"

"Tell Orlando that the reason he can't get through to his father is that he's too much like him," Ernesto said, laughing.

Orlando grabbed the phone out of Naomi's hand. "I heard that, dude, and I'll get you for it," he said. But Ernesto could tell he was laughing too.

At school the next morning, Ernesto spotted Naomi. "Hey, babe … everything okay at home?" he asked.

"Yeah, you calmed the troubled waters,

Ernie. When we got home from Hortencia's, Dad was mellow," Naomi said.

"Naomi, your father told me something I didn't know about Richie. I was in Los Angeles when his mom died, and I guess her murder was heavily covered in the local papers and on TV. Your father said Richie saw his mom get shot. Did you know that?"

"Yes," Naomi said. "When it was first reported on TV, they said the boy was in the car with his mother, and when she got out, her husband yelled something and shot her and then ran. When the police came, Richie was kneeling by his mother. I talked to Richie's foster mom. She said Richie has never talked about it. The only thing Richie has ever told her about his father was that he wasn't a monster."

"He told me that too," Ernesto said.

"One newspaper reporter called Richie's dad a monster, and some of the neighbors called him that too. Mrs. Loranzo was apparently well liked at church and in the *barrio*. I think some of the neighbor kids where Richie used to live called his father a monster for what he did," Naomi said.

"It's hard to imagine going through something like that for a kid … he must have been—what? Twelve or something?" Ernesto said.

"I think so, about that," Naomi said.

"Any clue ever come out why the guy did it? Not that there could be any excuse for something that horrible, but you wonder why," Ernesto said.

"There were rumors that Richie's father suspected his wife liked another guy. Everybody who knew her said that was ridiculous, but he was very suspicious and jealous," Naomi said.

As Naomi and Ernesto walked toward their first classes, they saw a small, noisy knot of freshmen standing on the pathway. Penelope Ruiz was in the midst of them and she screamed, "Angel Roma! Did he *really* sign that? I mean honest and truly did he sign it? It's not a stamp, is it?"

"I saw him sign it," Angel said. "Look what he wrote!"

Penelope read the words out loud: " 'To *mi amiga* Angel Roma.' Ohhh," Penelope cried, "I want one too!"

Penelope spotted Naomi and came running over. "Naomi! You gotta get me an autographed picture of Orlando too. When he comes down again, you'll get it, okay?"

"Okay, Penny," Naomi said. "Promise. How's your dad?"

"He's doing physical therapy, and Abel took him fishing. Dad used to love to go fishing, and he hasn't been in years! It's totally crazy, but that horrible car accident helped him in a way," Penelope said.

Ernesto headed for AP History, and Naomi walked toward English. Ernesto tried to act as if nothing had happened in the class, which was taught by Mr. Joaquin "Quino" Bustos, but the sad fact was that it was Mr. Bustos's son, Basil, who had driven drunk and caused the accident that injured Abel Ruiz's father.

Mr. Bustos was a brilliant, demanding teacher. And he continued to teach with enthusiasm in spite of the sad events. His only son was now in jail, facing charges of driving under the influence and causing great bodily harm.

Ernesto felt sorry for Mr. Bustos. He had to be humiliated and heartbroken, but he didn't let it show. He was as dedicated and thorough as ever, and he did not short-change his students in the least.

Rod Garcia and a couple friends in the class had laughed about the incident and ridiculed the teacher for having such a "loser" son, but they never did that in front of Mr. Bustos. All the students in AP History had a healthy fear of their teacher. Ernesto overheard Rod saying to a friend, "The old guy must be flawed himself to have such a son. My dad always says 'the apple doesn't fall far from the tree.'"

Ernesto kept his silence, but he thought bitterly to himself about the time he saw Rod Garcia leaving a party; Rod had been drunk and shouldn't have been driving, but he was on his way to his car. Rod Garcia could have been in as much trouble as Basil Bustos if Rod's friends hadn't intervened and convinced him to let somebody else drive.

Ernesto wasn't arrogant enough to think he knew why kids made horrible, life-changing mistakes. He'd seen very bad things done by kids with good parents. He'd seen enormous decency and generosity in kids from horrible backgrounds.

It was hard for Ernesto to imagine tougher circumstances than those Paul Morales faced as a kid. Yet, for all his toughness and bluster, Paul had about as good a heart as anybody Ernesto ever knew. Ernesto had no doubt that Paul Morales would risk his life for a friend and never give it a second thought.

Ernesto came to the conclusion that every human being, no matter the hand they'd been dealt, had a choice. You treated other people decently, you tried to help when you could, you tried to use whatever gifts you had, or else you whined and got bitter and tried to make everyone else as sad and angry as you were.

That was one of the things Ernesto so admired about Naomi Martinez. It was no picnic to live with Felix Martinez. He bullied his wife and children even though he loved them. His bellowing rages disturbed everybody's peace. Yet Naomi reached out to help whenever something came up. She was the first senior to volunteer to be a mentor. Ernesto thought Naomi's soul was even more beautiful than her face

CHAPTER TWO

Rod Garcia stood outside his history class after the teacher, Mr. Davila, had left. "I'm telling you," he said to two friends, "this school is going downhill fast. We got a senile old man—Jesse Davila—teaching our class right here. It's laughable that a man his age is still forced on us.

"Then Quino Bustos doesn't know what he's talking about half the time in AP History 'cause his son is going on trial in that drunk driving thing. Our senior class president, the jerk Ernie Sandoval, he spends most of his free time hanging out with gangbangers or wanna-be gang dudes. He's either hanging with them or some ex-con. I see him riding around the *barrio* in that crazy van

19

with bad dudes like Cruz Lopez and Paul Morales."

"Only good thing about Chavez is the track team. Coach Muñoz is counting on us to take the regional championship again, and I'm gonna be the fastest guy on the track. My only real competition is Julio Avila, and he's such a piece of trash—with a father who's beggin' for liquor money on the street—that he's likely to crash and burn before long."

Until that moment, neither Rod Garcia nor his two friends saw Ernesto Sandoval standing nearby, hidden by the vending machine. Now, apple in hand, Ernesto approached them. "Boy, talk about Chavez going downhill. You guys, you got some school spirit. You got nothing good to say about anybody. Dissing the teachers, raggin' on your fellow seniors. Dudes, with boosters like you, Cesar Chavez High doesn't need any enemies," Ernesto said.

"Well," Clay Aguirre, one of Rod's friends, shot back, "it's the truth. Some people just can't handle the truth. You got any idea what it looks like when our senior class president is standing out there with gangbangers in baggy pants and hoodies, laughing it up over some dirty lowrider junk car? Half the time your homies are getting frisked by the cops. I'm ashamed to tell people I go to a school that elected somebody like *you* class president."

"Aguirre," Ernesto said in a cool, angry voice, "none of my friends are gangbangers. Paul Morales is the manager of an electronics store, and he's taking filmmaking classes in college. He got to go to the Sundance Film Festival in Park City, Utah, his work is so good. His brother works for Councilman Ibarra, and he's doing a great job. As for Cruz and Beto, they're finishing trade school, and they're doing fine. I'm proud of my friends, dude, *all of them*. They're going to make the *barrio* a better place."

"Yeah, your creepy tagger homies, Dom Reynosa and Carlos Negrete, splashed more ugly graffiti around the *barrio* than anybody. You need to be proud of that," Rod Garcia said.

"Those guys turned their lives around and painted that fabulous mural here at Chavez. When alums come, they want to pose in front of that mural. Cesar Chavez, Kennedy, all the farm workers. It's a masterpiece. All the local TV people did coverage on it. What's *wrong* with you guys? Can't you stand to see kids fighting an uphill battle against the bad stuff going on around here and winning? Aguirre, Garcia, your families are better off than most of the families whose kids are here at Chavez … You want everybody who isn't doing well to just sink into the sewer and disappear?" Ernesto said.

"Yeah, that'd suit me fine," Rod Garcia said.

"I'm with you, Rod," Clay Aguirre added. "The *barrio* would be lots better without any of these bums."

Ernesto glanced at Mira Nuñez. She had

dated Clay Aguirre for a while. But recently she seemed to be drawing closer to him again. "How about you, Mira?" Ernesto asked. "You're a smart chick. You buying all this garbage these two are spouting?"

Mira shrugged. Her own mother was going through a series of bad relationships with loser boyfriends. She was setting a bad example for Mira. Clay Aguirre was handsome, and he was playing winning football for the Chavez Cougars. He could be charming when he wasn't being abusive.

"I don't know," Mira said, glancing at Clay for approval. "I don't like to see guys in hoodies and stuff, you know. They seem to be looking for trouble."

Abel Ruiz came along then. He looked at Ernesto and said, "Me and Dad are going fishing again Sunday. He's so excited. Like a little kid."

"That's good, man," Ernesto said.

"Hey, Ruiz," Rod Garcia said, "how come you hang with Sandoval? You're not like the rest of his friends. You're not a wanna-be gangbanger."

Abel looked Rod Garcia right in the eye. "You wanna know why I hang with Ernie? Because he's the best friend I ever had. He's my brother, man. He's got my back, and I got his. He's the best thing that ever happened to me at Cesar Chavez High School. You want more reasons?" He turned then and walked away. Ernesto caught up to him a few yards away.

"Creeps," Abel said darkly. "You think any one of them would volunteer for anything around here? Imagine Garcia or Aguirre signing up to tutor other seniors or to help a freshman kid who needs a buddy. Bunch of selfish creeps. If dudes like that ever become the majority, the planet is doomed."

Ernesto said, "I don't see you with Bianca Marquez so much anymore. You used to hang out with her."

"We still do," Abel said. "But Bianca is so hung up on what she weighs. I take

24

her someplace, and she doesn't want to eat anything. She just wants salad without chicken or fish or anything with protein. She thinks she's a rabbit who can live on lettuce."

Ernesto shook his head. "She's so thin anyway. What's with her?"

"She looks at all these skinny freaks on TV and in magazines. She wants to be like them. Her mother doesn't help either. She's just skin and bones, and she thinks it makes her look younger. The truth is it makes her look horrible. I'm telling you, Ernie, chicks can drive a guy crazy. My uncle Pete, he always says 'Women! You can't live with 'em, and you can't live without 'em.'"

Ernesto laughed.

"I, like, went nuts when Claudia dumped me," Abel said. "And that chick down where I work at the Sting Ray, Cassie Ursillo, she thinks I'm on my way to becoming some famous celebrity chef, and so she wants to date me. She's just like Mom. Whatever poor dude gets her is gonna be like Pop, just waiting for orders. And Bianca, she's fun and all that, but all the time counting calories. I think I'd be better off with a dog."

After school that day, Ernesto and Naomi were walking to the parking lot when Clay Aguirre barreled past in his new blue Hyundai.

"Hey, dude," Ernesto yelled, "not so fast! You wanna kill somebody?"

Clay looked out the window and yelled back, "Eat my dust, fool."

"Oh," Naomi said. "Mira is with him. He's wormed his way back in her good graces."

"Maybe him getting that brand new car has something to do with it. Clay's parents must be crazy buying him a Hyundai Equus. Most of us are driving beaters, and he's showing off in a car like that. He's asking for trouble," Ernesto said.

"Yeah, dudes with sharp objects might just want to redecorate that car," Naomi said.

"I'd like to do it myself," Ernesto said, "but, like, Clay is always throwing in my face that I'm a goody-goody, and I don't do stuff like that."

"I wouldn't love you if you did, Ernie," Naomi said.

Ernesto turned to Naomi and smiled. "If that's not a good reason to stay on the straight and narrow, I don't know what is," he said.

Clay Aguirre and Mira Nuñez went to the multiplex theater in the mall to see a movie. It was a movie about automobile racing that Clay liked and Mira hated, but she didn't say anything negative. In fact, she told Clay she loved the movie. The movie ended at eleven thirty. Clay and Mira both lived in the newer development off Washington Street, but they needed to drive all the way down Washington to get to their homes.

As Clay drove past Hussam's twenty-four-seven convenience store, Mira noticed the lights on. The store was mostly dark, but she could see a light shining from the rear, where something seemed to be going on.

"Look, Clay," Mira said. "I think somebody is in there." There was a shiver of fear in her voice. "Hussam once told me he never comes around the store at night. His wife is afraid to be home alone in their apartment with the kids, so he always closes around nine thirty and goes home."

"Let's cut down the alley and see what's happening," Clay said. Clay drove slowly down the alley with his lights off. "Look, babe," he cried in an excited voice. "There's Cruz Lopez's van parked right behind the store! The back door is half open! Oh man, Ernie's gangbanger friends are robbing Hussam's store. I bet Cruz and Beto are both in there. Probably Paul Morales too." Clay's voice throbbed with excitement. "I bet David Morales is in there too. They're all burglarizing the store. David got busted before for robbing stores at night. He's back in business, babe! Oh man, this is great.

We came by at just the right time. Now the cops can trap all the little rats at one time. Cruz, Beto, the Morales boys, they'll all get busted at once. They're all in there helping themselves to Hussam's stuff."

Clay Aguirre grabbed his cell phone and called 911. "Some punks broke into Hussam's twenty-four-seven store. It's on Washington Street … two sixty-eight Washington. Burglary going on right now. At least four guys in there. They're taking stuff out the back and loading it in the van. You better get over here fast. I know the guys who're pulling it off. Gangbangers. One of them is a parolee …" Clay looked at Mira and grinned. "I can't wait to see Ernie's face after this. He won't be so high and mighty about his homies."

Clay pulled farther down the alley and parked. He was close enough to see what was happening but wouldn't be in the way when the police cruisers came swarming in. Still grinning, Clay punched in Ernesto's cell phone number.

"Yeah?" Ernesto said. Although he was dead tired, he was still studying for Grace Lauer's English test, which was scheduled for tomorrow.

"Bad news, Sandoval," Clay said gleefully. "Cruz and Beto got their van pulled up behind Hussam's store. They're robbing the place. I think the Morales boys are here too. All your homies—the ones you're so proud of—they're down here cleaning out Hussam's store, dude. I called the cops. I hear the sirens now. A big bust is going down, man. Next time you want to hang with your homies, you'll be talking to them through a jail grill, dude."

Ernesto felt like somebody had just hit him in the stomach with a bag of cement. "No," he gasped, "they wouldn't be doing that. There's gotta be some mistake."

"Dream on, Sandoval. The cops are coming. I see the lights. They're gonna get all the rats red-handed. They'll be running for their lives, but it won't work 'cause the cops are coming down both ends of the alley. They're trapped like fish in a barrel. Sandoval, it's gonna be all over Chavez tomorrow. Our senior class president lost all his homies in one night 'cause they were out burglarizing a store!"

Ernesto was sick and stunned. Cruz and Beto robbing Hussam's store? Those guys were friends of the man! And Paul and David? It was like some crazy nightmare that couldn't be happening. Ernesto cut off Clay and called Paul Morales.

"Paul," Ernesto said in a shaky voice.

"You woke me up, dude. Wassup?" Paul said.

"Clay Aguirre just called. He said Cruz's van is parked behind Hussam's twenty-four-seven store, and he and Beto are carrying out stuff. He said you and David were there too. He called the cops and they're arriving," Ernesto said.

"That low-down jerk," Paul hissed.

"Is David there with you, Paul?" Ernesto had to ask.

"Yeah, but he's asleep," Paul said.

"Listen up, Ernie. It's not what it looks like. I'm swinging over to your house right away. Cruz and Beto need us there. Will you come with me?"

"Yeah, sure," Ernesto said, "but what's going on?" His whole body was numb.

"Dude, it's not what it looks like," Paul said. "I'll be at your place in five minutes."

When Ernesto put down the phone, his father was in the doorway. He was up late too, correcting tests. "What's going on, Ernie? You're pale as a ghost."

"Clay Aguirre called. He said Cruz and Beto and the Morales boys were burglarizing Hussam's store right now. Aguirre called the cops, but Paul said nothing like that was going on. Paul is gonna pick me up in a coupla minutes, and I'm going over there with him. We've got to help Cruz and Beto."

Luis Sandoval's eyes narrowed, and his mouth formed a grim line. "*Mi hijo*, if a burglary is going on, I don't want you in the middle of it."

"Paul said it wasn't a robbery. I don't know what's happening, Dad, but I gotta go with Paul and help my friends," Ernesto said desperately.

Seconds later, Paul swung into the Sandoval driveway in his Jaguar and hit the horn. When Ernesto and his father stepped outside, they saw Hussam, in his pajamas and a robe, also in the car. Paul had apparently gotten the man out of bed.

As Ernesto and his father got in the Jaguar, Paul said, "There's no robbery. It's all a stupid mistake. Aguirre had to know it wasn't a robbery, the dirty, rotten—I'll get him for this."

"Shelves," Mr. Hussam muttered in a dumbfounded voice. "I need more shelves high up. My store is so small. Had to go up. The boys, Cruz and Beto, they gave me a good price to build the shelves. Said they had to do it at night because they have classes at the college … I don't understand what is going on. I just wanted some shelves."

When they reached the alley, they saw Cruz and Beto in handcuffs, surrounded by police officers. When one police officer spotted Paul's Jaguar, he shouted, "Turn around. Police action going on here."

Paul's face was red with rage. He started to leap from the car when Luis Sandoval grabbed his shirt from behind. "Paul, let Mr. Hussam and me handle it, for the love of heaven!"

"Get back in your car," a police officer ordered as Ernesto's father slowly got out.

Luis Sandoval and Mr. Hussam stood beside the car with their hands in the air. Luis Sandoval said, "I'm Luis Sandoval, a teacher at Cesar Chavez High. This is Mr. Hussam, the owner of the twenty-four-seven store. There's been a terrible mistake. The boys were building shelves for Mr. Hussam."

Two officers came up to Ernesto's father and Mr. Hussam and frisked them for weapons. Then a police sergeant appeared. He looked at Mr. Hussam. "Are you the owner of the store?" he asked.

"Yes, sir. It is my store. I hired Cruz Lopez and Beto Ortiz to put in shelves. I have a very small store. There is no room, so I must put stuff up higher." Mr. Hussam was shaking with fear. He came from a country where nobody with any sense trusted the police. He thought he might be arrested or even shot before this night was over. He had not been in America long enough to trust the police.

The police sergeant looked perplexed. He conferred with another officer. It seemed what Mr. Hussam was telling them was what the boys said earlier when they were taken into custody.

"So you are saying the two young men were in the store tonight with your permission doing work?" the police sergeant asked.

"Yes, building shelves. I am a poor man. I cannot hire expensive people. The boys said they would do it cheap. They are … my friends," Mr. Hussam said, clutching his robe around his thin shoulders.

Ernesto glanced down the alley. He saw Clay Aguirre outside his car, taking this all in. Clay looked elated at the police action, but slowly he was beginning to look confused.

CHAPTER THREE

It took another thirty minutes for the police to complete their reports. Paul sat at the wheel of his Jaguar looking like he was about to explode. His features were disfigured with hatred. But he didn't move. Ernesto sat beside him, and if Paul had tried to get out and join the discussion, Ernesto would have grabbed him and held him.

When the police officers took the handcuffs off Cruz Lopez and Beto Ortiz, Clay Aguirre leaped in his car and backed out of the alley so fast that his tires squealed.

One by one, the police cruisers left the scene. It was all a mistake, but it wasn't the police officers' fault.

"That filthy punk," Paul raged to Cruz

and Beto. "Clay Aguirre called the cops the minute he saw the van and told them you were robbing the joint. He coulda checked in two seconds by calling Mr. Hussam."

Cruz was surprisingly mellow about it. "Well, we got most of the shelves done, Mr. Hussam. If it's all right with you, we'll just keep going and finish tonight. Then we'll load up the shelves, and you'll be good to go in the morning."

"I am so sorry this happened," Mr. Hussam said. He looked at Paul and said, "When you recommended these boys, I was so happy. They are so nice and polite." He turned to Ernesto and said, "I went into the electronics store to get some games for my sons, and Paul and I got to talking about my need for shelves, and he told me about these nice boys, and they gave me a good price. I am so sorry they had this trouble on account of me."

"It wasn't your fault, Mr. Hussam," Paul said. "Thanks for coming, man ..." His gaze went to Luis Sandoval. "Thanks a lot for coming along too, Mr. Sandoval. I think you saved the day."

"Yeah," Ernesto said. "If you'd jumped from your car and rushed the cops, you might be in the morgue now with a tag on your toe."

"Something like that," Paul admitted with a grim smile.

Paul drove Mr. Hussam back to his apartment and then took the Sandovals home. "Poor old Hussam," Paul chuckled, "I almost dragged him out of bed to come along. His wife was cursing me in Arabic."

"Paul," Luis Sandoval said as they neared Wren Street. "You gotta watch that temper. You're a good guy, but you're too quick on the draw. I know it hurts to see your friends suffering for something they didn't do, but one rash action can be cata-strophic. Those police officers are right on the edge. We lost two fine officers already this year, and these guys know how quickly a situation can turn deadly."

"Yeah," Paul said, "I hear you." But then

a dark smirk came to his lips. "I wouldn't be too surprised if Clay Aguirre ran into a spell of bad luck one of these days, though."

"No, Paul," Ernesto's father said. "See? You're not paying any attention to anything I said."

"I didn't say I'd do it, Mr. Sandoval. I'm just talking about karma, you know? The good that you do, and the bad that you do, it sorta comes around. Karma," Paul said with an evil glint in his eyes.

"You know, Paul," Luis Sandoval said, "you can learn a lot from your brother, David. He learned the hard way to straighten out. I was talking to Emilio Ibarra the other day, and he said David is the best thing that ever happened in that office. No matter how whacked out people are when they come in there with their grievances, David calms them down. Learn from him, Paul."

When Ernesto and his father walked in the house, Maria Sandoval was standing there, a look of alarm and anger on her face. "It's two in the morning! What on earth is going on? You two fly out of here like madmen without a word of explanation and I'm worried sick!"

"I'm sorry, Maria," Luis Sandoval said, embracing his wife and kissing her. "We should have called you. It all happened so fast. Clay Aguirre saw some of Ernesto's friends inside Hussam's twenty-four-seven store, and he called the police, said they were robbing the store. The boys, Cruz and Beto, were putting in shelves for Mr. Hussam. It was a horrible mix-up. Paul got poor Mr. Hussam out of bed, and Mr. Hussam explained to the police what was going on. When Paul got there, Cruz and Beto were in handcuffs … but everything is okay now."

Mom frowned. "Isn't it bad enough we have to deal with all the drama in the Martinez house without having to deal with Paul's weird friends? Good grief, sometimes I think I live in a madhouse. I like Paul Morales, he's a good person, but he has those strange friends."

"I know, Mom," Ernesto said, "but Paul is my friend, and so are Cruz and Beto. When Paul asked me to go with him to help those guys, I had no choice, Mom. They're my *amigos*."

Mom sighed. "I know, I know. It's just … oh, skip it. Speaking of problems, I ran into Susan Trujillo at the supermarket today, and she was all upset. She said her son was dating Mira Nuñez, and he was so happy in the relationship. Now Mira dumped Kenny, and she's back with that creep Clay Aguirre. Susan said her son is just crushed. He'd bought Mira a lovely gift for her birthday, and he thought everything was going along fine, and then Mira told him she was still in love with Clay. What an idiot that girl is!"

Ernesto didn't know Kenny Trujillo well. He was a nice, quiet kid who made good grades and worked as a box boy in the supermarket. Ernesto had seen Mira and Kenny at school, and they seemed to always have their arms around each other. Ernesto assumed Mira had wised up and seen Clay for the jerk he was, but apparently not.

"Clay just got a great new car, a Hyundai Equus. Maybe that's what turned Mira's head," Ernesto said.

"Oh my gosh," Ernesto's mother said, "are his parents nuts? Those cars cost a fortune. Like fifty thousand or something. Most of the kids at Chavez are driving old, used cars. They're too poor to afford anything else, and the Aguirres are letting their son flaunt that car? That is just ugly. Even if they can afford it, which I guess they can, it's just going to make a lot of kids hate Clay even more than they already do."

"Yeah," Ernesto said. "I hope somebody messes up the car."

Mom turned sharply. "*What* did you say, Ernie?"

Ernesto backtracked quickly. "Uh, I just said maybe somebody is gonna be so jealous they'll, you know, mess with the car … you know, like key it or something."

"But *you* wouldn't do anything like that, would you, Ernie?" Mom demanded.

"No, no, of course not," Ernesto said, thinking to himself that he had to fight his bad instincts to avoid doing something much worse to Clay after what he did tonight.

"Kenny Trujillo was in my history class last year," Luis Sandoval said, drinking the coffee Ernesto's mother had just made. Maria Sandoval figured the night was shot anyway and they might as well have coffee. "Nice guy. I can't imagine a smart girl like Mira dumping him and going back to Clay. Clay Aguirre doesn't know how to treat a girl." He shook his head. "When I see these girls taking so much bad behavior from guys, I think we need a class in middle school that would teach girls to have enough respect for themselves and make good choices. There's this ongoing problem of girls picking bad boys, and then you get into domestic abuse, and around and around it goes."

"I never was attracted to bad boys," Maria Sandoval said, a wry look on her face. "I steered clear of them in school, and then I fell for this really boring guy who was good as gold and treated me so nicely. It didn't hurt, either, that he was the hottest dude I'd ever seen. Ernie, did I ever show you pictures of me and your dad at the beach while we were dating ... he had these abs that just gave me goose bumps."

Ernesto grinned at his father, who was smiling and turning a little red. "You still look good, Dad," Ernesto said. "I showed those pictures you're talking about to Naomi, Mom, and she goes 'oh *that's* where *you* get that ripped look!'"

Luis Sandoval was a darker shade of red, but he was still smiling.

When Ernesto saw Clay the next morning at school, he walked over and said, "That was such a rotten thing you did last night, Aguirre. I never even thought *you'd* do something that disgusting. You knew those guys in the van were friends of Paul's and my friends too. You could have called either of us, and all of that hassle could have been avoided."

"I thought Paul Morales was one of the criminals robbing the store, Sandoval. I'm gonna call *him* and say I'm about to call the cops?" Clay snarled. "I did the right thing, man. I did what any good, law-abiding citizen would have done. I see these criminals in a store in the middle of the night and I figured they were robbing the joint."

"Aguirre, Cruz and Beto aren't criminals, and you know it," Ernesto snapped.

"I don't know it," Clay Aguirre said. "All your homies are low-life creeps. They probably were about to steal stuff and the only reason they didn't was because the cops showed up. You hang with trash, Sandoval, and a lot of people are sick of it. You think everybody loves you here at Chavez, but a lot of kids hate your guts. I'm not the only one. Now you even got criminals from the ninth grade under your wing, lousy little bums like Bobby Padilla and Richie Loranzo. Padilla was a runaway … and Loranzo's old man is doing time for murder. What kind of scum is that? How come you don't like to hang with decent people?"

"Aguirre, if you're a sample of what you call 'decent people,' then I want no part of them," Ernesto said in a savage voice. "You don't seem to have a heart, man."

"You don't have a brain, Sandoval," Clay snapped. "If you want to hang with homies, with criminals, then maybe those are your own kind."

Ernesto walked away just as Mira Nuñez was coming. He cast her a dark look. "I thought you had more sense, girl," he said in a low voice. "You got out of the spider's web once, and now you've jumped back in."

"You got him all wrong, Ernie," Mira said in a sincere voice. "He's changed. There's a lot of good about him now."

"I guess there's something good about

rattlesnakes too," Ernesto said. "I guess they eat rats. But Aguirre doesn't even do that, because he *is* a rat."

"That's very harsh, Ernie," Mira said in a hurt voice. "I didn't know you had that much bitterness in you."

Ernesto walked on to Ms. Lauer's English class and a test on poetry. Ernesto dreaded the test because he hated poetry. The only poem he ever remembered liking was one in his fifth-grade English book. He had forgotten who wrote it, but he had memorized it, and even now the sentiments of the poem were close to his heart. The title of the poem was "I'll Be There," and to Ernesto it described the way he felt about his homies:

> When the world has turned against you,
>   I'll be there,
> When the fates have seemed to doom you,
>   I'll be there,
> With fire at your back,
> And flood against your heels,

I'll be there,

If no one else is with you,

And you are all alone,

I'll be there,

At every start and end

Ever and forever,

I'll be there, my friend.

As he sat down at his desk, Ernesto spotted Kenny Trujillo looking as if his last friend in the world had died. Ernesto wasn't close enough to the guy to offer any words of encouragement, like he did to Abel Ruiz when Claudia Villa dumped him.

Apparently, Kenny thought a lot of Mira, and the end of their relationship was tearing him up.

Ms. Lauer passed out the test papers, and Ernesto noted with disgust that most of the questions pertained to the poetry of one of Ms. Lauer's favorites, Sylvia Plath. Plath left Ernesto completely cold, but he'd studied her because he suspected this was coming.

During the test Ernesto wrote the stuff he had gleaned during his study. When Ernesto was almost finished, he noticed that Kenny Trujillo had stopped writing. He just sat there, a blank look on his face. He probably hadn't studied much. He was too busy mourning the loss of Mira.

When Ernesto went to Jesse Davila's history class, he was concerned, as always, that Rod Garcia and his friends would catch the poor teacher in another gaffe and restart the drumbeat against him. One of the oldest teachers at Chavez, Davila was coping with his wife's Parkinson's disease and helping to support a single daughter and her child, Angel Roma. He had so much on his plate that it was no wonder he made some mistakes in his lectures.

Ernesto and most of the other students were more than willing to cut the poor man some slack, but Rod Garcia was ready to pounce at any misstep.

Last night, Ernesto's father had mentioned Mr. Davila's problems. Luis

Sandoval said he'd spent some time with Mr. Davila, and they had worked out some new lesson plans for him. Ernesto thought his father sounded pretty excited about it. Dad really wanted to help his colleague. Ernesto got the impression that his father felt toward his friends on the faculty a lot like Ernesto felt toward his homies. He wanted to be there for them too.

"I think Jesse is going to surprise everyone," Luis Sandoval said, sounding and looking like the cat that just swallowed the canary. "His detractors might just be flabbergasted."

Ernesto thought Dad had given Mr. Davila a good pep talk or something. He didn't know how much good that would do.

Mr. Davila walked into the classroom and said, "I'm sure you people all know about Skype."

"Oh man," Clay muttered under his breath, "the old fool is dabbling in technology now; he doesn't have a clue!"

"Shut up," Ernesto hissed softly at Rod Garcia and Clay. They were both snickering mockingly.

"Today we are going to have a visit from a rather important person, a woman who once served as secretary of state for the United States. She has a wealth of knowledge about America as a world power," Mr. Davila said.

"Now he's hallucinating!" Rod gasped.

"We will be able to see and hear Madame Secretary, and she will see and hear your questions," Mr. Davila said.

Ernesto noticed the big computer screen in the front of the classroom. Suddenly the woman who once served as secretary of state appeared. She smiled and said, "Good morning to the students in Mr. Jesse Davila's American history class. I am happy to be visiting you at Cesar Chavez High School although I am quite a few miles away. So I invite your questions. Identify yourself and ask your question."

Ernesto immediately raised his hand.

"Madame Secretary, I am Ernesto Sandoval. I remember seeing pictures of you on television when you served as secretary of state. I often wondered if the fact that you were a woman and men usually served in that office made your job more difficult. Did other world diplomats have any problem with dealing with a woman?"

The former secretary of state laughed and said, "Well, Ernesto, they may have had problems, but I never let them bother me. Actually, you ask a good question. At first, some of the male diplomats seemed reluctant, but as soon as we started discussing our common interests in world peace and prosperity, I found even men from different cultures and a diverse view of the role of women were quite gracious and forthcoming."

"I'm Janet Diaz," a girl said, "and I'd like to ask what your most challenging foreign policy issue was."

"Well, Janet," the woman said, "they are all challenging, but as secretary of state

I found the problems in the Middle East to be most difficult. We have been trying to resolve differences in that part of the world well before even *I* was born, so you can imagine how long that was." The class broke into laughter.

The questions went back and forth during the period, which seemed to fly. The students were really excited about an opportunity to talk to someone they knew as an important member of the government, someone they had seen discussing important matters with all the anchors of the television networks a few years ago.

Ernesto noticed that Rod Garcia and Clay Aguirre did not participate at all. They looked dumbfounded. They could not understand how such a miserable teacher as they perceived Mr. Davila to be could have pulled something like this off.

Ernesto grinned to himself. Now he knew why his father was chuckling with such self-satisfaction last night.

At the end of the period, Mr. Davila

said, "Many thanks, Madame Secretary, for talking to our students today. Believe me, you have made this class a memorable one."

"Thank you, Mr. Davila," the woman said, "for giving me the opportunity to chat with such bright and attentive young people. My faith in the next generation has been strengthened."

CHAPTER FOUR

After class, Ernesto went up to Mr. Davila's desk and said, "Sir, that was a home run!"

Abel was right behind Ernesto. "You hit that sucker right out of the ball park, Mr. Davila," he said.

Janet Diaz gasped and said, "Nobody is gonna believe I was actually talking to a lady who used to be secretary of state!"

As the class filed out, everybody was talking about what just happened.

"How did he get somebody like her to go along with this?" Clay wondered. "You think she was an impersonator?"

"Aguirre, don't be even stupider than you already are," Abel snapped. "Did you see the guys from the TV station come in and take some video? This is gonna be on the news tonight."

Ernesto walked with Abel toward the vending machine. "My dad and Mr. Davila were brainstorming the other day about cool things they could do in their classrooms. I think this is one of the ideas they came up with. It's gonna help Mr. Davila a lot."

"It won't be so easy to make fun of him after this," Abel said.

Naomi came running over. "You guys! Angel just texted me! She said her grandpa is a big shot 'cause he got the former secretary of state to talk to his students."

"That's great, Naomi," Ernesto said. Angel Roma had had some rough times. While she assisted her disabled grandmother, some mean girls taunted her almost every day. The principal had dealt with the girls, and now Angel had some peace while she helped her grandmother.

Before Ernesto went to his next class, he got a text message from Paul.

"Can you come over after school? Carmen will be here too."

"Now what?" Ernesto thought. "See you, man," Ernesto texted back.

In the late afternoon, just before his last class, Ernesto got a text from Ms. Sanchez, the principal. He was already worrying about what was going on with Paul Morales, and now this.

"I'll need five minutes of the senior class meeting tomorrow, Ernie," Ms. Sanchez texted. "Real important."

"You're on the schedule," Ernesto texted back.

Ernesto wondered if there were complaints from disgruntled seniors that he didn't know about. Rod and Clay were always hinting at a vast reservoir of discontent with Ernesto's leadership. He didn't see it himself, but maybe it was percolating beneath the surface.

Maybe the senior tutoring program wasn't going as well as Ernesto thought. Maybe the seniors *were* resenting the mentoring outreach to freshmen. If he focused on the "'what-ifs" too much, Ernesto was very good at undermining his own self-confidence.

After the last bell, Ernesto hurried to his Volvo for the drive over to the Morales apartment. He earnestly hoped nothing was wrong there.

As Ernesto drove up to the apartment, he spotted Carmen's car. Maybe David had lost his job at Councilman Ibarra's office, and Carmen had come over to console him. Everything Ernesto had heard about David's job performance was great, but maybe something had come up.

When Ernesto hit the doorbell, David opened up. "Come on in, Ernie," he said, smiling. He didn't look unhappy, which was encouraging.

Ernesto smelled enchilada sauce. Paul emerged and said with a wry look, "Carmen is making green enchiladas. You gotta be the first to try one, Ernie. If you think it's edible, then David and I will dig in. But if they're so bad you get deathly sick, then we won't brother."

"I heard that," Carmen yelled from the kitchen. "It just so happens I am a very good cook. Not as good as Abel, but darn good."

"So, what's up?" Ernesto asked, still a little nervous.

"Well," Paul said, "I was simmering about what happened the other night. For my homies to be hassled like that for no reason just burns me up, dude. Aguirre knew what he was doing. So we're hatching a little plot to redecorate that Hyundai Equus a little bit. Word is that Aguirre and Mira are going down to Balboa Park Sunday and that'd be a good place—"

"Oh man, Paul," Ernesto groaned.

"Yeah," David said. "It makes me sick too."

Paul glanced at his brother. "Would you believe this guy who's been in the slammer for two years would have turned into a snitch? Yeah. He heard me and Cruz talking about our plans and he turned rat. He told on me, Ernie," he said.

David looked at Ernesto and grinned, "I called your dad, Ernie, and told him to talk to Paul before he got in trouble."

Ernesto remembered last night his father leaving the house in a hurry. He said he forgot some papers at school. It sounded weird, because Dad rarely forgot anything, but Ernesto didn't spend too much time thinking about it.

"Luis Sandoval showed up here last night, Ernie," Paul said. "He came in all his glory. I haven't been dressed down so bad in all my life. He yelled in my face. I saw a side of your father I've never seen before. He said I had a bad life as a kid but that was no excuse for me to mess up now. He said if I damage Aguirre's car, he'd tell the cops and get me busted. He really said that."

Ernesto looked closely at his friend. Paul Morales did not take criticism well. He was a tough customer. Ernesto wondered if he was angry at Luis Sandoval.

"Ernie," Paul said, "I never had a father. I had a mom for a little while, but she wasn't much good because of the drugs. But I never had a father. When Naomi talks about her old man yelling and laying down the law, I think 'Hey, I never had that. I never had some strong man who cared about me taking me down.' I guess what I'm saying is this, Ernie. Thanks for loaning me your father when I needed one."

Ernesto was swept with relief. "You're not doing it then … you're not vandalizing Aguirre's wheels?" he said.

"I've gone to Plan B," Paul said. "I'm making a doll that looks like Aguirre, and I'm sticking pins in it and putting a curse on him."

Carmen emerged from the kitchen with a baking dish filled with chicken-and cheese-stuffed tortillas and green chili verde sauce. There was sour cream on the side.

"You're darn right he's not messing with Aguirre's car," Carmen said. "Not if

David and I have to tie him to his bed. I love this crazy dude, and he's gonna stay out of trouble, or I'll tear that curly black hair right out of his head."

When Ernesto tried the enchiladas, he had to admit that Abel could not have done better.

The next morning, Ernesto was still putting the finishing touches on the agenda for the senior class meeting today. His cell phone rang.

"Ernie," Naomi said, "Mira Nuñez just called me. She said she and Clay went to a movie at the mall last night and when they got back to the Hyundai, somebody had let the air out of all their tires!"

Ernesto felt dizzy. Paul had sounded so sincere about not messing with Aguirre's car, and now this? Luis Sandoval had gone to all the trouble of talking some sense into Paul, and Paul seemed to be really getting it, and now this? "Naomi, I was just over at Paul's yesterday, and he said he wasn't going to do anything like that. I believed him, babe."

"Mira told me it was so horrible. They were stuck down there until after midnight getting the tires fixed. Clay is sure Paul is behind it," Naomi said.

"Naomi, I'll get back to you," Ernesto said. He called Paul's apartment. David had already left for work, and Paul was taking a last gulp of coffee.

"Paul, Mira Nuñez called Naomi. She and Clay were out at the mall last night, and somebody let all the air out of their tires," Ernesto said.

"Not me, dude. Not Cruz or Beto either. I swore to your father I'd stay clean. My homies promised me they would too," Paul said.

"Okay, Paul," Ernesto said.

"You believe me, right?" Paul asked.

"Man, you've always been straight with me," Ernesto said. "I believe you. But Clay is raving that it had to be you and your friends retaliating for the other night."

"Maybe some punks just saw that ritzy car sitting there and decided to have some fun," Paul said.

"Yeah," Ernesto said. He called Naomi back. "Paul swears he had nothing to do with what happened to Aguirre's car, Naomi, and I believe him. A lot of guys hate Clay. When he plays football, he's so brutal. He hit a guy from Lincoln in that last game, and it was so bad I thought he'd get called on it. And then he faked being injured, dropping down and crying in pain, but it was just a ploy. He was up and going strong in the next play. A lot of guys resent him."

"Yeah," Naomi said, "and he taunts kids at school too. Even on the road, he flips out other drivers all the time. I saw him in a road rage incident once. He cut some guy off so bad there was almost an accident."

"Well, thanks for the heads up, Naomi. See you at school," Ernesto said.

In the morning, Clay Aguirre was waiting for Ernesto. As he parked his Volvo,

Clay came storming over. "You hear what your dirty homies did to my car last night?" he yelled in Ernesto's face so close that Ernesto felt his hot breath.

"My friends had nothing to do with that," Ernesto said. "Paul swore to me he didn't mess with your car and neither did Cruz and Beto."

"And you believe those dirty criminals?" Clay shouted. "I'm reporting what happened to the cops, and don't be surprised if your homie buddies go to jail after all."

"You're crazy, Aguirre," Ernesto said, walking away. As he did, he noticed a commotion going on in the freshman area. Abel drove his little sister, Penelope, to school every day, and today, right after he let her out of the car, she ran to join about ten other freshmen.

Abel sat in his car watching his sister, a smile on his face. As Ernesto approached, Abel said, "She's going nuts, Ernie. She's freakin' out, man."

Penelope saw Ernesto and she ran

toward him. "Ernie, Ernie, I got it!" she screamed. "I got the picture. It's just as good as Angel's picture. He wrote on it, 'To *mi amiga* Penelope Ruiz,' and he signed it!" Penelope waved the colored photo of Orlando Martinez. "He's even cuter in *my* picture than he is in Angel's picture!" She almost shoved the picture into Ernesto's face. "Don't you think so, Ernie? Isn't he the cutest dude you ever saw?"

"Uh, well ... maybe," Ernesto stammered.

"It came in the mail," Penelope said. "He said he couldn't come down for a few weeks, but he wanted me to have the picture. Isn't that sweet? It was addressed to me. *To me!*"

"Wow," Ernesto said.

"Naomi must have told him about me," Penelope said. "Oh, I love her so much."

"Me too," Ernesto said.

"Ohhh, Ernie, he looks just like he does on his Facebook page. Don't you think so?" Penelope cried. "I'm gonna post a message on his wall. I'm gonna tell him how much I love his *ranchero* music. This is so awesome."

"Come on, girl," Abel growled. "Get to your classes. You wanna be late and get detention?"

Abel looked at Ernesto. "You can look superior, dude, but your time is coming. Before you know it, Katalina is gonna be a teenager, and this is what it's like. It's like an evil spell overtakes them."

"Hey, Abel, somebody let all the air out of Clay Aguirre's tires last night while he and Mira were at the movies. He's blaming Paul and his friends, but they didn't do it," Ernesto said.

"Couldn't happen to a nicer guy," Abel said.

"That's how I feel, too, but he's telling everybody Paul Morales and Cruz and Beto did it. That makes me sick," Ernesto said.

"Clay Aguirre is a real dog, man. So many people hate him that it coulda been any one of a coupla dozen. Or maybe it was just some dude who didn't even know him, somebody who resented a guy having a brand new car when most of us are driving cars older than we are. They see this young dude tooling up in a car like that and, well ..." Abel shrugged.

Ernesto tried to concentrate on his classes during the day, but he kept wondering why Ms. Sanchez wanted to talk at the senior class meeting. He kept thinking it had to be something bad.

Ms. Lauer returned the English tests. Ernesto's grade was a B-plus. He wanted an A. It didn't matter because he had a strong A in the class already. He figured his loathing for Sylvia Plath's poems must have showed in his essay.

When the time came for the seniors to gather in the auditorium, Ernesto's stomach was hurting. When he worried a lot about something, it always happened. Deprise Wilson, the bubbly senior class advisor, smiled at him as usual and fell in step beside him as he walked to the auditorium. Ernesto wondered if Ms. Wilson knew why

Ms. Sanchez requested five minutes to address the seniors today.

"Ms. Sanchez texted me," Ernesto said, fishing for information. "She wants to talk to the seniors today."

"Really?" Ms. Wilson said.

"Yeah, I hope everything is okay," Ernesto said.

"Oh, I'm sure it is," Deprise Wilson bubbled. "Everything has been going swimmingly." She was young and cute and bursting with optimism. She looked more like a senior herself instead of the advisor and an art teacher. Unlike Ernesto, she consistently looked on the bright side of everything. Ernesto thought if a tsunami struck the school, she would smile and say "Well, at least the campus got a good cleaning."

As Ernesto walked toward the stage in the front of the auditorium, Clay Aguirre came up alongside him and said in a low, vindictive voice, "Another chance to mess up, Sandoval. Go for it. Maybe you'd like to start an outreach to the other drug addicts who live in the ravine at Turkey Neck. Yeah, that'd be a good idea. Each senior could adopt a homeless drug addict."

Ernesto ignored Aguirre and continued walking toward the stage. Ms. Sanchez was already up there, which made Ernesto even more nervous. He had always gotten along fine with Ms. Sanchez, and he tried to tell himself that if there really was something wrong, wouldn't she have talked it over with him before telling the whole senior class?

"Before we begin today," Ernesto Sandoval addressed the seniors, trying to hide his nervousness by gripping the podium, "our principal, Ms. Sanchez, would like to speak to us for a few minutes." Ernesto turned toward Ms. Sanchez and smiled. Then he stepped back.

"Thank you, Ernesto," Ms. Sanchez said, coming to the microphone. "I'm so pleased to see so many of you here today. It seems there are more students every time we have a senior class meeting, and that's a good sign that you're interested in your school's student government. But I came here today to talk about our two programs just recently instituted at our school. These programs have generated a lot of comments and interest.

"First, we have started a senior-to-senior tutoring program here at Chavez. Seniors who are having trouble academically or even in other ways are now able to get another senior to help them along. The seniors who are having problems in class could always seek tutoring from the teachers, but this senior-to-senior plan is new.

"Secondly, we have started a mentoring program, where seniors reach out to at-risk freshmen. Seniors who wish to volunteer get a little brother or little sister from the freshman class, and they do activities together. The seniors help their freshmen with their studies and also arrange for social activities.

"Both of these programs sound wonderful. But are they working? I now have an assessment of just how these programs are going …"

Clay whispered something to Rod Garcia. Both sneered at Ernesto. They were sure the principal was about to drop a bomb on Ernesto Sandoval's head.

CHAPTER FIVE

For the first time since I've been principal here at Cesar Chavez High School," Ms. Sanchez said, "there are no seniors in danger of failing. We attribute this to the aggressive efforts not only of our excellent teaching staff, but to this wonderful program of seniors helping seniors. Somebody once said it takes a village to raise a child. Well, that's true, and it takes a whole student body to make sure every student makes it to graduation day."

The auditorium exploded with cheers and applause.

"Now, for the progress report of the mentoring project, the outreach to our ninth graders. Our ninth-grade teachers have told me that at this stage of the school year, there are a lot of youngsters dropping out. Many of our students, sadly, do not return for tenth grade. But the outlook for our ninth graders is brighter this year than ever before because kids who are faltering are being helped. Once again, our seniors are making us proud.

"We don't know how these programs will turn out in the long run, but right now we are excited and optimistic. So a great big thank you to all our wonderful seniors who have stepped up to the plate, and a special thank you to your dedicated senior class president, Ernesto Sandoval."

The applause and cheers that broke out seemed to rock the foundation of the auditorium.

Ernesto was almost at the parking lot to get his car and go home when he heard somebody following him. He turned to see Rod Garcia, his eyes narrow with anger. "That deal at the senior class meeting was such a crock," Rod said. "What's your secret, Sandoval? How did you get Ms. Sanchez to give you props like that?"

"What are you talking about?" Ernesto demanded. "I didn't even know what she was going to say. She asked to speak at the class meeting and that's all I knew."

"No way, dude. Everybody in the know thinks your stupid programs are going nowhere, and here's the principal acting like you're the best thing since double cheese on a burger. She's eating out of your hand, man. What's going on?"

"Ms. Sanchez doesn't eat out of anybody's hand," Ernesto snapped. "She tells it as she sees it."

"No way, Sandoval," Rod Garcia said, sneering. "She's hot, and I guess she likes it when a young, good-looking dude shows her a lot of attention. When you go in her office and sweet talk her, it must feel real good."

Ernesto saw red. He didn't have a quick

temper, but this time the blood rushed to his head, and before he even knew it, he had grabbed Rod's shoulders and backed him hard against the chain link fence. He gave Rod Garcia a violent shake and spat out the words, his spit showering Garcia's face, "You dirty little punk. Don't you *ever* say anything like that again! Ms. Sanchez is a fine woman, and she's probably old enough to be my mother. I respect her deeply, and she treats me just like she treats everybody else. If you ever *dare* imply otherwise, I might smash your face in no matter what it costs me."

Shock and horror transfixed Rod Garcia's face. He never expected Ernesto Sandoval to react in such a violent way. When Ernesto let go of him, Garcia staggered backward. When he recovered his balance, he took off fast in another direction, moving even faster than he did in the track meets. Ernesto's heart was pounding.

Seconds later, Naomi came along. Even from a distance as she approached Ernesto, she could tell that something was wrong. "Ernie, what's the matter?" she asked. "You look so … so strange."

"It's been a full day," Ernesto muttered.

"Babe," Naomi said in a soft voice. "Ms. Sanchez just praised you to the skies at the meeting, and I'd think you'd be over the moon …"

"I just almost smashed somebody's face in," Ernesto said.

"*What*?" Naomi gasped.

"It's a long story, babe. I *will* tell you about it, but not now. My heart is beating so fast I can't talk too well. Okay?"

Ernesto often felt superior to Paul Morales when it came to controlling his temper. But right now he felt he was about the same. He was disappointed in himself, and yet he didn't regret it either.

"Ernie, let's stop on the way home for a mocha," Naomi said. "I need for you to talk to me now. I gotta know what's got you so upset. I won't sleep tonight if you don't tell me because I'll be imagining all kinds of terrible things."

Sitting in the little coffee shop, Ernesto said, "I almost smashed Rod Garcia's face in. In another minute I would have broken his nose, so it'd be sideways in his face. I never knew I could get so mad so fast. It scares me, Naomi. I could have done major damage."

"But you stopped yourself, Ernie," Naomi said. "That's the important thing."

"Garcia, he so desperately wants me to fail as senior class president. It's all the guy thinks about. It's been eating at him. He was so sure Ms. Sanchez would tell the seniors that the programs of seniors tutoring seniors and the mentoring project for the freshmen weren't working. He was counting on her chewing me out for focusing on the wrong priorities. He wanted to hear her say the senior class is coming apart and it's my fault. Then when she said all those nice things, he freaked, Naomi. He cornered me in the parking lot and he …" Ernesto stared into his mocha.

"What, Ernie?" Naomi said, putting her soft hand over Ernesto's.

"He said me and Ms. Sanchez must have something going on for her to praise me like that. He said she was hot, and she and I got something going on," Ernesto said.

"Oh, Ernie, what a creep! Ms. Sanchez is such a straight arrow and you are too. Jealousy is making Garcia crazy," Naomi said.

"I wanted to do the guy serious harm, Naomi," Ernesto said. "I'm not sure I ever came that close to injuring somebody." Ernesto looked at Naomi. "Why couldn't I just be rational and see what he said for what it was, the pathetic ravings of a jealous loser? I am so disgusted with myself. I came close to maiming him and ruining my own life too. Last year, you remember those guys who got in a fight on the street, and one of them punched the other and he fell and hit his head and died? They weren't criminals. They were just young guys who lost their cool, and one ended up dead, and the others are in prison for a long time. *I came so close.*"

Naomi squeezed Ernesto's hand. "But, babe, you stopped yourself. You came close, but you stopped yourself. Don't you get it? You had the character and self-control to stop yourself from hurting him. You shouldn't be disgusted at yourself. You should be thankful that you were able to put the brakes on your anger. It's not what we *almost* do that brings us down, Ernie. It's what we are able to stop ourselves from doing that lifts us up."

Ernesto smiled at Naomi. "You make me feel a little better, babe. You always manage to do that. I guess I need to work out more, get rid of my aggressions."

"You don't have that much aggression, Ernie," Naomi said. "Just forget about the creep and enjoy the wonderful compliments you got today from Ms. Sanchez. When you ran for senior class president you promised you'd be looking out for all the kids, and you are. You're one of the good guys, Ernie, and, wow, do we need good guys."

When Ernesto got home, his mother rushed at him and gave him a big hug. "Oh, Ernie, I'm so proud of you I could bust. Conchita called me and said Carmen was at the senior class meeting, and Ms. Sanchez said such wonderful things about you and everybody clapped! Then Linda Martinez called and said the same thing. Naomi texted her right after the meeting. I must have gotten ten texts. Ernie, you're a true leader!"

"Thanks, Mom," Ernesto said. But, in spite of what Naomi said, Ernesto was still angry at himself for losing his cool so badly. Sure, he stopped himself from hurting Garcia, but was that because there was such terror on Rod's face? What if Garcia had made his dirty accusations over again? Would Ernesto have been able to stop himself from serious violence, then? That was a question Ernesto couldn't answer and that troubled him deeply.

When Ernesto passed Katalina's and Juanita's bedroom, Katalina was looking at her computer. Juanita was in the living room with *Abuela*.

"Whatcha looking at, Kat?" Ernesto asked, poking his head in the door.

"Isn't he handsome?" Katalina sighed. "That's Naomi's brother, Orlando. Ohhh, he's sooo handsome …"

Ernesto was alarmed. "No, no," he told himself. "She's only nine." Abel had warned him what was ahead for Ernesto's little sisters, but this was too soon!

"He's old, Kat," Ernesto said. "He's twice your age. He's probably going bald."

"He's not old," Katalina cried, giggling. "And look at his beautiful hair. Oh, I'd like to touch it! I love long hair on a boy."

"He's not a boy," Ernesto said. "He's a man." Ernesto was growing more perplexed. "He looks like a wild man with all that hair.

What kind of a man has such crazy-looking hair? Katalina, why aren't you playing with your dolls?"

"Ohhh, Ernie," Katalina said, tossing her head. "I don't play with dolls anymore."

"Yes you do," Ernesto said almost desperately. "I saw you playing with your dolls just a few weeks ago."

"That is so boring," Katalina said. "Look, it tells what new songs Orlando is going to sing. Ohhh, I love his songs."

"And your stuffed animals," Ernesto said in a plaintive voice. "Where is your nice teddy bear with the red ribbon around his neck?"

"I don't play with teddy bears anymore, Ernie," Katalina giggled. "I'm almost ten years old!"

"Nooo," Ernesto said. "You're many months from being ten. Many months. Where is he? Where's your teddy bear?"

"I put him in the closet," Katalina said.

"Is that nice? You put Tommy in the old, dark closet. I bet he feels bad in the closet.

He's probably crying," Ernesto said.

"Oh, Ernie," Katalina laughed, "you're being a big silly! Teddy bears don't cry."

"How do you know?" Ernesto demanded. He came into the room and opened the closet door. He saw Tommy on a high shelf. He took him down and cradled him in his arms. "I think I *do* see tears, Kat. Look, he's crying."

Luis Sandoval had come home from school and he paused in the doorway of his daughter's room, staring at Ernesto. "Hi, Ernie," he said, "why are you playing with Katalina's teddy bear?" There was a half smile on his face.

"She's mean, Dad," Ernesto said in a serious voice. "She stuck poor Tommy in the closet so she can watch Orlando Martinez on YouTube." Ernesto propped Tommy the teddy bear on Katalina's pillow where she used to keep him. "Now, Kat, you let him stay here, okay?"

"Okay," Katalina giggled. "Isn't Ernie a big silly, Daddy?"

Ernesto followed his father down the hall.

"I don't want her growing up too fast, Dad. She's only a little girl. I don't want her getting like Penelope Ruiz. I mean, I like Penelope and all that, but all she thinks about are guys and clothes and stuff," Ernesto said. "I mean, I just don't want Katalina growing up too fast."

"You and me both, *mi hijo*," Luis Sandoval said. Then he grasped Ernesto's shoulders and said, "Everybody at school is talking about the wonderful job you are doing. I am so proud of you."

"Thanks, Dad. The seniors—most of them—are so great. I couldn't do anything if it wasn't for them stepping up for everything," Ernesto said.

"By the way," Luis Sandoval said, "Clay Aguirre is ranting around school how somebody let the air out of his tires. He's blaming Paul and his friends, but I took Clay aside and made it clear to him that Paul and his friends had nothing to do with it. I swore to it. I think Clay believed me finally."

"Paul told me that you went over there and set him straight about any plans for revenge that he had," Ernesto said.

"I suppose he's ticked off that I did that but—" Ernesto's father started to say.

"No, Dad, Paul surprised me by saying he was grateful. He said he never had a father to set him right, and he said he didn't mind borrowing mine," Ernesto said.

"Did he really say that?" Luis Sandoval asked with a wide grin. "I'm telling you, that's a good kid there. A diamond in the rough."

On Saturday morning, Maria Sandoval peered into Ernesto's room as he was checking out a news story on his iPhone for his American history class.

"Ernie, I was planning to take Alfredo out for a stroll. It's such a beautiful day, but I'm kinda hammered for time and I was wondering ..." Ernesto's mother said.

Ernesto got up. "Sure, Mom," he said.

"Thanks! He's already all dressed and in the stroller. I even put his little Chargers football cap on him. He loves it," Maria Sandoval said.

Ernesto grabbed his own Chargers cap off the shelf and started pushing the stroller out the front door.

"Well, little guy," Ernesto said, "Mom's busy, and you're stuck with me."

Ernesto thought he had a kind of unusual family. Mom and Dad were very young when they married, and Ernesto came in the second year of the marriage. Then there were no more babies for a while. Mom thought Ernesto might be an only child. Ernesto's parents wanted a boy and a girl. Eight years after Ernesto's birth, along came Katalina, and then, two years later, Juanita. The Sandovals were so happy. They thought their family was complete and then, last year, along came Alfredo.

Alfredo gurgled happily as they reached the sidewalk. A butterfly swooped down and he grabbed for it, but it got away. Ernesto pushed the stroller down Wren Street, where the Sandovals lived, to Tremayne, the cross street. He turned right, on Bluebird, hoping to maybe see Naomi.

As Ernesto walked, he saw a lady coming from the other direction, carrying a small bag of groceries. He'd never seen her before. He knew most of the people who lived around here, but she was a stranger, nicely dressed with blue-white hair.

As they neared one another, Ernesto smiled and said, "Hi." He always did that. He couldn't imagine passing another person this close and not acknowledging them. He learned that from his parents.

Mom always said, "Maybe in New York it's the style to ignore strangers, but in the *barrio* it's not."

"Hello," the lady said in a pleasant voice. She looked right at Ernesto and then at Alfredo in his stroller. "My goodness," she said. "You look so young to be a father! You look like you're still in high school."

"Yes, I am," Ernesto said, beginning to explain, but the woman continued talking.

"Not that I'm being critical or anything, though I do think you young people are rushing things a bit. Nevertheless, I admire you for manning up and helping to care for your son. I don't live around here, but I've heard there are many single mothers, and the fathers don't stay around to help parent their children. So I do respect you for fulfilling your obligations."

"Ma'am," Ernesto finally got the chance to say, "he's my brother. Little Alfredo here, he's my brother. I'm not anybody's father yet."

"Oh, well, that's better," the woman said. "You are much too young for family responsibilities. My son had a girlfriend when he was sixteen, and she had a child, and my son just wanted nothing to do with the child. I mean, sixteen! Now my grand-daughter is living with her other grandparents. The child is fourteen now. Perhaps you know them. They live right down on

90

Finch Street. The Davilas. He's a teacher at Cesar Chavez High, a nice man. But the poor man's wife is very ill, and it's just an awful situation."

"Yes, Mr. Davila is my history teacher at Chavez. He's a great teacher," Ernesto said.

"Oh, really? Well, my name is Irene Roma. My granddaughter is Angel Roma. Poor little thing. She's wild and rebellious. I don't get to see her much. I don't know what will become of her. All my son left her was his name. My son has been just a dreadful disappointment, and probably the misbegotten child will take after him."

"I'm Ernesto Sandoval," Ernesto said. "And don't worry too much about Angel. She's doing okay. She's in a mentoring program with a great senior, and they've bonded beautifully. Angel is doing much, much better."

CHAPTER SIX

O h my goodness," the woman's face broke
into a smile. "I'm so glad I ran into you! My
daughter-in-law has remained very bitter
about what my son did, so we don't have
a good relationship. But Mr. Davila did tell
me that Angel had this friend at Chavez
High, a girl named Naomi, I believe. And
he said the girl had a boyfriend named
Ernesto, and that must be you!"

"Yes," Ernesto said.

"Oh, I am delighted to meet you! I've
heard such good things about you and
Naomi. Mr. Davila can't say enough good
about you two. Oh, I wish my son had been
like you, Ernesto. Jimmy got in fights in
school; he was always getting suspended.

What a treasure you must be to your parents!" Irene Roma said.

"Thank you, ma'am, but nobody's perfect," Ernesto said.

As Ernesto went on his way pushing Alfredo in the stroller, he thought about Jimmy Roma. Maybe one day he met somebody like Rod Garcia and there was a terrible fight and that was the beginning of a sad, downhill slide.

Ernesto turned down Bluebird Street. He saw Naomi's gold car in the driveway, which meant she was home. Ernesto felt a rush of happiness. Whenever he thought of seeing Naomi, he felt happy.

Felix Martinez was out in the front yard mowing grass. "Look at all the weeds, Ernie," Mr. Martinez said. "But they're green, right? So I mow 'em and let 'em be. As long as they're green. Idiot next door, he's spraying weed killer all the time. Poison. Then he waters the lawn and the poison goes down to the bay, right? Idiot." Felix smiled then. "Hey, cute little *muchacho* you got there, Ernie. Look how big he's getting. Seems only yesterday he was getting born. Enjoy him. They grow up fast. Seems like yesterday I had three cute little *muchachos* of my own playing baseball with me in the park. I was Pop, the big shot. Then they grew up, and they give me grief most of the time. They ain't my sweet little *niños* no more."

"You got pretty nice boys, Mr. Martinez," Ernesto said. "Orlando and Manny are doing good in the Latin band, and Zack seems to be okay being with them up there. Even my little sister, Katalina, she's always looking at Orlando's picture online."

"Ahhh, I got my troubles, Ernie. They don't respect me no more. They're the big shots now, and I'm just the jerk who runs a forklift. Orlando comes down and calls me a *bobo*. Would you call your father a *bobo*?"

"Well, no," Ernesto admitted, but in truth, Luis Sandoval was not like Felix

Martinez. Mr. Martinez and his sons had violent fights and for a long time the sons were estranged from their parents. It took Ernesto and Naomi working together to bring the family back together.

Mr. Martinez was often rude and gruff with Linda, his wife. That bothered Orlando and his brothers, and Ernesto didn't blame them for being angry. Ernesto couldn't even imagine his father being rough or rude with Mom. Still, Ernesto thought Felix Martinez was basically a decent guy, and he felt affection for him. He was the father of the girl Ernesto loved—Naomi.

"Well, you guys get along pretty good most of the time, Mr. Martinez, and I know your sons do love you. I don't doubt that for a minute."

"I ain't so sure," Felix Martinez said, turning off the mower. He came closer to the stroller and looked at Alfredo. "He looks like you, Ernie. Gonna be a good-looking kid. Hope he's as good as you are, Ernie. And speaking of that, you're really wowing them down at Chavez. When Naomi told me you were running for senior class president, I wasn't so sure you could pull it off. I thought if you bombed it'd be hard on your old man, him working as a teacher there. But you aced it, Ernie. Congratulations."

"Thanks, Mr. Martinez," Ernesto said just as the front door of the house opened and Naomi came out.

"Ohhh, you got the baby with you," Naomi screamed, hurrying over. "Oh, may I hold him? He's so cute!"

"Sure," Ernesto said. "I think he likes girls already. He smiled the minute he saw you."

Alfredo seemed most content with his mother, *Abuela*, Naomi, or even Penelope holding him.

"Isn't he a doll, Daddy?" Naomi cooed.

"Yeah," Felix Martinez said. "Wait'll he's older. Little kids, little problems. Big kids, big problems. I know plenty about that. You're okay, Naomi, but your brothers …"

Ernesto's cell phone rang. It was Mira Nuñez. She had dated Clay Aguirre last year, but his abusive personality drove her away. Now she was back with him, which made Ernesto and all Mira's friends sick.

"Ernesto, you've got to do something about that horrible gangbanger Cruz Lopez. He rides back and forth in front of Clay's house, in that monstrous, garish van, just taunting him. Clay is so steamed," Mira said.

Days earlier, Cruz and his friend Beto Ortiz were doing work at Hussam's twenty-four-seven store at night, and Clay thought they were robbing the place. He called the police and the boys got hassled. It enraged Paul Morales, who was close with Cruz and Beto. In angered Ernesto too. All Clay had to do that night was check with Ernesto and the police bust never would have happened. Ernesto could have told Clay the guys were doing work in the store for Mr. Hussam. But Clay Aguirre was so anxious to make trouble for Ernesto's friends. He never forgave Ernesto for taking Naomi Martinez away from him last year. Clay never blamed himself for losing Naomi. His rudeness and physical abuse drove her off before Ernesto started dating her.

"Look, Mira, tell Clay to ignore Cruz. The streets are public. Cruz can drive the van up and down if he wants. They're still mad that Clay got the cops down on them the other night, but they won't damage his car or anything. Tell Clay his stupid Hyundai Equus is safe. They won't damage it. He should just ignore them and they'll go away," Ernesto said.

"Ernie," Mira said, sounding as if she were crying. "It's getting to Clay … I mean, can't you *do* something?"

"Mira, those dudes, Cruz and Beto, they were just working that night, and Clay called the cops, who cuffed and almost arrested them. I'm sure they're just letting off some steam, for crying out loud," Ernesto groaned.

"Ernie, Clay, and I were doing so good.

He wasn't like he was before, last year, kinda mean and stuff. He really was being nice to me and it was wonderful, but now, it's like they're tormenting him, like a bug that keeps buzzing you, and you can't get away from it. Ernie, *he's started taking it out on me*. Please, Ernie, can't you make them stop?"

Ernesto rolled his eyes and sighed. "I'll see what I can do, Mira," he said. Naomi put Alfredo back in the stroller, and Ernesto headed home.

Ernesto was revolted by the thought that a smart girl like Mira Nuñez continued to date a creep like Clay Aguirre. Clay was a bully. If things weren't going his way, he took it out on the most vulnerable person he could find. It was Naomi for a while. And now it was Mira.

Ernesto figured Cruz Lopez was behind the harassment. Beto usually just went along with whatever Cruz thought up. That's how it always was. Cruz was the stronger and tougher of the two. They'd been buddies since they rode skateboards in the *barrio* as nine-year-olds, and they were inseparable. They were also close friends with Paul Morales, Ernesto's close friend. Paul had a tattoo of a rattlesnake on his hand to honor the time he was almost fatally bitten in the desert and Cruz and Beto carried him to medical help, saving his life.

Ernesto drove to the Lopez house, where Cruz lived with his widowed father and two younger sisters. The wildly painted van was parked out front. The family had gone through a lot in the past year. Cruz's father was out of work and lost his health insurance just as his wife fell ill. By the time he was working again and she could get medical help, her illness had become deadly.

Ernesto would never forget the sad little Lopez family in Our Lady of Guadalupe Church at her funeral.

Now, thanks to Ernesto's father's intervention, both Cruz and Beto were learning building trades at City College. It seemed both boys were on the right track.

When Ernesto rapped on the door, the whole flimsy place seemed to rattle. Cruz answered.

"Hey, Ernie, what's going down?" he asked.

"Can I come in, man?" Ernesto said.

"Anytime, homie," Cruz said. "Welcome to our slum."

Mr. Lopez was at work and the two girls were visiting their friends. The house had worn furniture with the stuffing oozing out of some of the chairs. Duct tape was wrapped around some of the worst tears. Ernesto remembered when the family was so poor that the only food they had came from Abel, Paul, and Ernesto. Now that Mr. Lopez was working again, things were much better.

"Cruz, we got a problem," Ernesto said.

"Shoot, homie," Cruz said. "If it's something I can help with, you know I will."

"You and Beto been making Clay

Aguirre crazy driving back and forth in front of his house, dude," Ernesto said. "You get real close to that fancy car."

Cruz grinned. "We get close, but we never hit it," he said. "It's a public street. He got us hassled for no reason, and if we can do something legal to yank his chain, why not?"

"Yeah," Ernesto said, "but Clay is going ballistic."

"Poor baby," Cruz said, an evil grin on his face.

"Cruz, he's got this sweet girlfriend, Mira Nuñez, and he's taking out his frustration on her. She begged me to try to stop the harassment for her sake. Clay can't get at you guys, but he's making her life miserable."

Cruz's expression darkened. "Ernie, you ever have your hands cuffed behind your back?"

"No, can't say as I have," Ernesto said.

"You ever have cops screaming at you to get down on the floor … and wondering if maybe you're gonna get shot by mistake or something?" Cruz asked.

"Okay, man, you made your point," Ernesto said. "You hassled Aguirre. You had your fun, now knock it off. Do it for the chick. Do it as a favor to me. For one thing, it's not smart for you guys to be doing stuff like that anyway. Pretty soon you'll be out of school and looking for jobs. You gotta grow up, homie."

Cruz shrugged. "Okay, Ernie. I remember you and Abel lugging lots of eats into this house when we were hungry. Me and Beto were having fun screwing with Aguirre, but for you, we'll call it off," he said.

Ernesto grabbed Cruz's hand. "*Gracias,* homie," he said.

When Ernesto got back to his Volvo, he called Mira.

"Yes?" she said, her voice still high and shaky.

"Mira, Ernie here. I talked the guys into stopping what they were doing," he said.

"Oh, thank you, Ernie," Mira cried. "I knew you'd help me."

"Mira, why don't you dump this idiot?" Ernesto said impatiently. "Remember when you told me your mom was dating some ugly jerk who was mistreating her, and you talked your mom into getting some backbone? You helped your mom toss that fool out. Then you got the guts to dump Aguirre, and now you're back with him again. You remind me of a fly who gets caught in a spider's web, and a gust of wind shakes the web, and the fly gets away only to hurry back into the web. What's with you, girl?"

"Ernie, you don't understand. I love Clay. He's not like he used to be. He treats me nice, unless he's under a lot of pressure, like when the boys were bothering him. That brought out the old Clay, but most of the time he's really sweet. He does nice things for me and stuff. I mean, after all the big changes he's made, it just broke my heart that he kinda reverted to …" Mira said. "I mean, Ernie, don't you believe that people can change?"

"I guess so," Ernesto said. "But it doesn't happen too often."

"Well, thanks a million for helping me, Ernie," Mira said.

"Yeah," Ernesto said, starting the Volvo and heading home.

Ernesto promised Richie Loranzo, the freshman he was mentoring, that he'd go over to his house on Monday afternoon and help him with his algebra homework. Ernesto had already met the couple who were Richie's foster parents, Sam and Arlene Bejaraña, but he hadn't spent much time with them. He really hadn't gotten a feel for them yet. They were in their fifties, a nice, quiet, kindly appearing couple who had raised their own two children. Now they wanted to help a foster child. They had both retired from professions, so they didn't need the money the county provided, though they received it.

"I was never very good in math myself,"

Mr. Bejaraña told Ernesto when he arrived at the house. "I'd like to have been able to help the boy, but what little I learned in school myself back in the day, I've forgotten."

"Same with me," Arlene Bejaraña said. "I always hated arithmetic. Couldn't even get the grasp of long division. If you can believe that. Working at the barber and beauty shop was really good for Sam and me."

On the walls of the modest frame house on Sparrow Street were many pictures of the Bejaraña children as they grew up. Their school pictures were displayed, along with their graduation and wedding pictures.

"We have a boy and a girl," Arlene Bejaraña said. "Now they live a ways up the coast. They're doing fine, though. We're glad for Facebook. We can see their pictures and get updates of them and the grandkids."

Ernesto went into the small bedroom where Richie slept. There were still photographs of the Bejaraña son on the wall. Richie had a bed, a chest of drawers, and a little bookcase that was filled with comic books. Richie also had a desk with a small computer.

"This is pretty cool, Richie," Ernesto said. "Do you use the computer a lot?"

"Yeah," Richie said. "I play games."

"And look at those comic books. You collect them?" Ernesto asked.

"Yeah, I got a lot of Spider Man. He's my favorite. I got him when he's fighting all kinds of bad guys. I like Sandman and Dr. Octopus and the Chameleon the best." He looked at Ernesto with his sad brown eyes. "Do you like Spider Man, Ernie?"

"Yeah," Ernesto said. "He was kind of a shy guy in real life, and then when he transformed into Spider Man, he got a lot of courage. It had to be fun to be able to do that."

They worked on Richie's algebra homework for more than an hour. Ernesto was not great in math, but he could easily handle freshman algebra. Because he had to struggle himself as a freshman, Ernesto was able to thoroughly grasp the concepts, and now he could make it clear for Richie. Several times, Richie's eyes lit up and he cried, "Oh yeah, yeah, now I get it!" Those were moments that Ernesto treasured. He recalled his own "a-ha!" moments when an elderly lady tutor had helped him out.

When the homework was done, Ernesto approached the Bejarañas and asked, "I noticed a little hamburger place on the corner. They got a special on cheeseburgers. Would it be okay if Richie and I walked down to get a couple?"

The couple smiled and nodded.

As Ernesto and Richie walked down to the corner, Richie said suddenly, "I like you." His face flushed red when he said that, and he quickly looked down at his sneakers, as if he'd revealed too much of himself.

Ernesto threw an arm around the boy's shoulders and said, "I like you too, Richie. You're a nice kid."

They kept on walking. The boy seemed to be fidgeting, as if he wanted to say something but didn't know quite how to say it. Finally Richie said, "They were fighting over the gun."

Ernesto felt his heart pump a little faster.

The foster couple said the boy never mentioned the circumstances of his mother's death. He never said a word. He never spoke about it at school either. He was given the opportunity to talk to grief counselors, but they said he just sat there in grim silence.

"Your parents were fighting over a gun, Richie?" Ernesto asked gently. He thought it would help the boy if he finally was able to talk about the night his father shot his mother to death, and he was left an orphan without an immediate or extended family.

When the police and paramedics came to the Loranzo house, they found the boy sitting on the floor with his dead mother; the father was in a state of shock.

"Yeah," Richie said. "Mom, she wanted

to leave. Dad couldn't get a job. Mom said he was lazy. She wanted to leave."

"Lot of people can't find jobs," Ernesto said.

"He got the gun to scare her. He had it hid in the garage. He didn't want to …" Richie's voice trailed.

"I understand," Ernesto said.

Ernesto got the picture now. The man was out of work, and the woman was at the end of her rope. If her man couldn't support her and their son, she wanted out. But the man didn't want to let his family go, so he got the gun and hoped in some crazy way he could force her to stay.

"Mom tried to take the gun away from him," Richie said. The boy hung his head and shook a little. Then he said, "It went off. *Bang*. Like that." Richie reached up and covered his ears. "*Bang*," he said again.

Tears were running down the boy's face.

"She wouldn't wake up. She never would wake up," Richie said. "I begged her

to wake up." The boy dried his tears on h
sleeve and they continued walking.

They got a booth way back in the corner
of the hamburger place. They ate their
cheeseburgers and drank some soda, and
then Richie looked at Ernesto and said, "He
didn't mean to hurt Mom. He didn't mean
to. Do you believe me, Ernie?"

Ernesto nodded. "Yes, Richie, I believe
you," he said.

CHAPTER SEVEN

It was the first round of the playoffs, and bitter rivals Lincoln High and Cesar Chavez High were pitted against each other. Ernesto Sandoval and Naomi Martinez filed into the Chavez Stadium wearing warm jackets and Cougar logo caps. Ernesto wasn't the biggest football fan in the school by any means, but he was senior class president, and he'd already caught heat for not being sports-minded enough. He had to show his colors now.

Ernesto really did want the Cougars to win, even though Clay Aguirre was on the team, and he'd probably get some of the glory. Mira Nuñez was on the cheerleader squad, and she looked happy. Ernesto figured Cruz Lopez had stopped harassing Aguirre and things were cool with Clay and Mira again.

In the first quarter of the game, Lincoln drew blood, scoring a touchdown. A wild cheer rose up from the Lincoln fans. A groan of concern erupted from the Chavez fans.

As Chavez advanced the ball in the second quarter, Mira Nuñez and the other cheerleaders danced and screamed, "Go, Cougars, go!" The Cougar defense lined up to keep the ball in their possession as they headed for the end zone. Clay Aguirre was the best linebacker, and due to his aggressive plays, the Cougars were able to score their first touchdown, which tied the score seven to seven.

The cheerleaders, led by Mira chanted, "Clay, Clay, you saved the day!" Mira was in her glory.

Ernesto had to admit Aguirre looked good out there. He was big and tough, and when he was helping to advance the ball, he was formidable. The Cougars scored another touchdown before the second quarter ended, and they headed into the third quarter on top, fourteen to seven.

Ernesto and Naomi looked at each other. They had to smile at Mira's wild joy. She was almost defying gravity in her joyous jumps. She couldn't have looked happier if she'd just been chosen Miss America.

"She really loves the dude," Ernesto said ruefully to Naomi. "Go figure."

"Totally," Naomi agreed. Sadly, she understood better than anybody what Mira was feeling, because once Naomi loved Clay too. He could be charming and endearing when he wanted to be, and then, when things went wrong, he turned ugly. There was something romantic and wonderful about Clay, and Naomi had thrilled to see him playing football. But then he was rude. And finally he was physically abusive, and it was over.

When Naomi met and fell in love with Ernesto, she realized that what she had felt for Clay wasn't the deeply satisfying love she felt for Ernesto. She didn't know it at the time, but what she felt for Clay was wild and glorious infatuation with a very bad boy.

"Poor Mira," Naomi thought now.

The whole stadium seemed to hold its breath when Lincoln threatened to score in the fourth quarter. Then the Lincoln player fumbled the ball, and Clay Aguirre got into the end zone for the winning touchdown.

It had turned into Clay Aguirre's night, and he was enjoying every minute of it.

"He's quite an athlete," Naomi admitted as the stadium exploded into joyous celebration. Chavez had taken the game twenty-one to seven. The Chavez Cougars would advance to the next level in the championship games.

Mira Nuñez ran out to embrace Clay, and he lifted her into the air, kissing her. Her screams of joy pierced the night.

Ernesto and Naomi arrived in the parking lot at the same time as Clay and Mira.

Ernesto was really sorry about the timing. Unfortunately, they were close enough to see each other, and Ernesto thought he had no choice but to acknowledge Clay's fine performance in the game. "You made history tonight, dude," Ernesto said. "You ran thirty-two yards into the end zone with that last TD. You were the man."

Clay stopped in his tracks. He looked stunned. It was the last thing he expected Ernesto Sandoval to do. Clay's mouth opened, but no words came. He seemed to be waiting for some zinger, to take the wind out of the compliment. Only Mira said, "Thanks. We're all so proud of him."

While Clay Aguirre was still trying to figure out how Ernesto's compliment was something of a dig that he didn't get yet, Ernesto and Naomi drove past the Hyundai and Ernesto called out, "It was one for the books, man."

Naomi laughed as they drove down Washington Street. "Ernie, you never cease to amaze me. That was so incredibly cool.

Poor Clay, he just can't recognize that kind of gallantry. It's so far from the way he thinks," she said.

"I can't stand the guy, but he was great tonight and he deserved props," Ernesto said.

"I like that, Ernie," Naomi said. "I shudder at people who hate so deeply that they have these deep, lasting grudges. Life is too short for that kind of stuff." Then Naomi turned her head and said, "Look, Ernie … Kenny Trujillo came to the game. I'm surprised he would. He's really been missing Mira, and to see her out there cheering for another guy … I didn't think we'd see him tonight."

"Yeah," Ernesto said. "I always felt funny about Mira and Kenny. He's a nice guy, but he's nerdy. Mira seems to like a lot of excitement, football heroes, guys with cool wheels. Like she'd never have gone for me. I'm really lucky to have found a wonderful chick who doesn't mind a dull dude in a Volvo."

Naomi gave Ernesto a playful poke in the ribs. "Babe, you're hotter than the grand finale at the fireworks show on the Fourth of July, and don't you forget it," she said. "Besides, I like the Volvo."

At school on Monday, Ernesto saw Kenny Trujillo sitting alone on one of the stone benches near the science building. In the year and a half that Ernesto had been a student at Cesar Chavez High, he'd maybe talked to Kenny three or four times, and that was usually about a test that was coming up. Still, Kenny was a senior, and he looked despondent, so Ernesto walked over and said, "Room for me at the end of the bench, man?"

"Sure," Kenny said in a listless voice.

"Saw you at the game Friday night," Ernesto said. "Some game, huh? I guess we're still in the chase."

"Yeah, I like the Cougars," Kenny said. "But I wanted us to lose."

Ernesto knew where he was coming

from, but he didn't want to come right out and say it. "Got to do with a chick, eh?" Ernesto said.

"Yeah, me and Mira Nuñez were doing good. I couldn't believe a chick like her liked me. I thought I'd died and gone to heaven. I thought she was so done with that Aguirre creep, but then he turned on the charm and won her back. How do you compete with a jock? It was like taking candy from a baby, him taking her away from me," Kenny said in a forlorn voice.

"It happens, man," Ernesto said.

"Ever happen to you?" Kenny asked, looking right at Ernesto.

"No, but when I first met Naomi Martinez, she and Aguirre were tight. I had to work really hard to win her over. I'm not sure I ever could have if Aguirre hadn't treated her so bad," Ernesto said.

"Clay Aguirre is no good for Mira," Kenny said. "Right now he's being nice, but he'll turn on her sooner or later. My dad was like that. Sweet as sugar when he was getting the breaks, but when life turned sour, he made Mom's life miserable. She finally kicked him out. Life at our house got a lot better after that."

"Man, Kenny, I don't know what to tell you. Mira got sick of the dude once before. She told him off in front of everybody. You remember? She yelled at him, and we all applauded. I guess you gotta wait for her to come to her senses," Ernesto said.

"That's so hard. I see them together, and it's like I'm one big wound, and somebody is pouring on salt and I'm burning with pain," Kenny said. "If I could think of a way to make Aguirre revert back to his old ways … to get him so riled up that Mira would finally see him for what he is."

"Well, don't play with fire, dude," Ernesto said. "You can't orchestrate something like that. It could backfire. You never know what might happen. You gotta have patience, Kenny. Show Mira you got class. If you guys are meant to be together, it's gonna happen for you."

120

Kenny said nothing. He just stared into space. Then the first classes of the day were about to begin, and both boys took off.

In the middle of the week, Mira Nuñez was having lunch with Clay when she got a text message. She looked startled and Clay leaned over and read it.

"IWALU," the message read.

Clay frowned. "Who's writing junk like that to you, babe? Where's this 'I will always love you' coming from?" he demanded.

"Oh, Kenny is having a hard time with us breaking up, Clay," Mira said. "He'll get over it. Don't let it bother you."

"It *does* bother me," Clay snapped. "Tell him to drop dead. I don't want some idiot like Trujillo sending text messages to my girlfriend, okay?"

"I'll just text him back that it's over between us, and he shouldn't bother me anymore," Mira said.

"He better not. I outweigh him by fifty pounds. I'll wrap the little jerk around a palm tree," Clay said.

"Don't text me anymore," Mira texted. "We're over."

"Not strong enough," Clay complained. "You shoulda told him to drop dead like I told you."

"He'll back off now," Mira said. "Oh, Clay, I'm still over the moon about the game Friday. The cheers were so loud in the stadium. Did you read the online sports page? They're talking about you maybe being recruited by some of the big colleges as the best linebacker on the West Coast. One guy commented, 'Meet the next Heisman Trophy winner!'"

The frown left Clay's face and he grinned. "Yeah, that was pretty cool. You know what blew my mind, Mira? That jerk Ernie Sandoval, he congratulated me. He's got an ego as big as an elephant and even *he* was impressed," Clay said.

"Yeah," Mira said. "You were awesome. Everybody at Chavez is impressed."

"Last year I was in a slump, babe, but I'm hitting my stride now. But I never thought Sandoval would be in my cheering section," Clay said.

"Ernie's not a bad guy, Clay. He'll give credit where credit is due even if he's not friends with the person," Mira said.

Clay darkened a little. "The dude is a pain. Ever since he got senior class president, he acts like he's king of the world. Well, I'm putting that dude in the shade. I hope the school newspaper starts covering sports more instead of featuring the monkey business Sandoval is up to. Now that the Cougars are in the hunt to be regional champs, we should get a lot of print. That's what the kids want to read about, not soupy drivel about do-good junk," Clay said.

Mira made the huge mistake of saying, "Bianca Marquez told me that the senior-tutoring-senior thing has helped her a lot.

She was almost flunking out of two of her classes until Ernie started tutoring her."

Clay's eyes narrowed. "What's with you, babe? You got a crush on Sandoval or something? All you can do is say nice things about him," Clay growled.

Mira laughed. "Oh, Clay, I was just so happy that even he recognizes how great you are. I mean, when somebody like Rod Garcia says you're awesome, you expect that 'cause he's a friend, but for Ernie to be so gushy, I mean, it just made me so proud that the guy I love is now loved by the whole school!"

Clay smiled. "Yeah, I get it. You're right, babe. When we even got Sandoval cheering, we've got it made," he said.

Deep in Mira's heart, she was saying nice things about Ernesto Sandoval because of what he had done for her in calling off Cruz Lopez's harassment. Mira would never share that story with Clay. Clay believed that the harassment had stopped because of the threats he had yelled at Cruz. Even though Mira loved Clay Aguirre, she knew he would never do what Ernesto had done. In moments when truth invaded Mira's soul with a cold, clear light, she admitted to herself that Ernesto Sandoval was a better person than Clay. But she was hopelessly in love with Clay, and nothing else mattered.

Usually Clay drove Mira home, but today he had football practice, so she took the bus. As she was nearing the bus stop, Kenny Trujillo approached her.

"Mira," he said, "I need to talk to you."

"Please, Kenny. Don't make it hard on me. You know how jealous Clay is. Everything is going so well now with me and Clay. Don't screw it up for me, Kenny. If you really care about me, you'll want me to be happy, and I'm so happy with Clay now," Mira said.

"I do care about you, Mira. I love you. I'm sick that we're not together anymore. I can't sleep. I can't eat. My mom is yelling at me that I'm losing weight. I'm messing up in my classes. Last time you got sick of Aguirre, I was there for you right away. Remember when you said you weren't gonna take his abuse anymore and I—" Kenny spoke in a trembling voice.

"Kenny, leave me alone. Clay and I are fine now. He's a different person than he was last year. I'm sorry you're hurting, Kenny. I didn't mean to hurt you, but I just never got over Clay, and I had to see him again. You and me, it was just a temporary thing. I knew I belonged with Clay. Just leave me alone, okay?" Mira said. Kenny stood there as the bus pulled up to collect the students from Chavez. Just before she boarded the bus, Mira turned back one more time and said, "I'm sorry, Kenny, I truly am." Then she disappeared into the bus and the doors closed.

Abel Ruiz was on his way to his car when he overheard part of the conversation between Mira and Kenny. Abel knew Kenny a little better than Ernesto did. They had more classes together. They were both in speech class, and they had worked together on a major report.

Abel knew what had happened between Mira and Kenny. Now he walked over to Kenny and said, "Dude, listen up. It happened to me too a few weeks ago. I was crazy for this chick like you wouldn't believe. I woke up every morning thinking about her, and I went to sleep every night thinking about her. Then she dumped me like a hot potato, right out of the blue."

"But, Abel, how do you get over something like this?" Kenny asked in a bewildered voice. "How do you, you know, get through it?"

"A friend of mine, a guy who's a little older, he helped me a lot, Kenny. I was really freaking out and this dude said, 'be calm, be cool, and don't let her see you bleed.' That's what you're doing wrong, man. You're groveling. Chicks lose all respect for you when you grovel. Maybe that creep Aguirre will go toxic on her again, and she'll want to get back with you if she has some respect for you. Personally, though, I wouldn't take her back, but maybe you'll want to," Abel said.

"Did your chick come back, Abel?" Kenny asked.

"No, the dude she dumped me for dumped her, and we both decided to go our separate ways. I got over it, man. It's like with zits. It's miserable for a while, but it goes away. I hang with Bianca Marquez now. No big thing. We just have fun. You'll find somebody like that too, Kenny. Just pretend there's a big wind blowing, and you're hanging on for dear life. But then the wind stops, and you're still there. My friend, his name is Paul. He gave me some great advice. Going through this is gonna make you stronger, Kenny. You'll be okay," Abel said.

Kenny Trujillo didn't say anything. He appreciated that Abel Ruiz wanted to help him. Ruiz was a good guy. But Kenny thought Abel must not have loved his chick like Kenny loved Mira. He couldn't have gotten through it like he described if he had loved her that much.

Kenny Trujillo believed that he loved Mira about as much, if not more, than any dude ever loved a girl, and he couldn't stand the thought that he was losing her. He just couldn't.

Kenny had to do something that would make Clay Aguirre see who he really was. Something that would make Clay so mad that he would turn into the ogre he was down deep. Kenny had heard the story of how, when Clay was dating Naomi Martinez, he hit her so hard that her entire face was bruised for days. That was who Clay was.

Kenny had to show that side of Clay Aguirre to Mira so she would see the light before it was too late. Then Mira would understand what a terrible mistake she'd made going back to Clay and turning her back on someone who really loved her—him.

Kenny thought Mira would come back to him then, and everything would be all right again.

This time she would be over Clay Aguirre for good.

Kenny noticed a ninth-grade boy waiting for his parents to come pick him up. He was big for his age and tough looking. Kenny knew his name was Rocky Salcedo, and he had the reputation of being a bully. Ms. Sanchez, the principal, had come down hard on Rocky, so he wasn't bullying other kids as much, but Kenny thought he would be just the kid to help him now. Kenny walked over to Rocky and said, "Wanna make ten bucks?"

Rocky grinned, "Yeah!" he said.

Kenny handed him his cell and dialed the number of Clay Aguirre's cell. He told Rocky what to say.

"I seen Mira Nuñez with Kenny last night," Rocky said. Then he turned to Kenny. "Where's my ten?"

Kenny stuffed the bill into the boy's hand.

CHAPTER EIGHT

Maria Sandoval's parents came down from Los Angeles to visit the Sandovals on the weekend. Ernesto loved Alfredo Vasquez, his mother's father, for whom little Alfredo, the newest Sandoval, was named. Eva Vasquez, his mother's mother, Ernesto did not like as much. Eva Vasquez never made a secret of the fact that she thought her daughter made a mistake in marrying Luis Sandoval instead of pursuing her own career, which was bright with promise.

When Grandfather Vasquez spotted his little namesake in his stroller, Chargers baseball cap on his little head, the older man beamed with joy. Last night when they called, Maria Sandoval had promised her father that if the weather was nice, he could take the baby for a walk. Now, in the bright, sunshiny morning, Alfredo Vasquez took charge.

"Look how he's smiling at me," Mr. Vasquez said with delight. "I think he already knows I'm Grandpa."

Ernesto's mother was so happy that her father was eager to be a part of the little boy's life. Luis Sandoval's father had died some years ago, and the Sandoval children needed a grandfather.

Ernesto had been named for his father's father, and though Alfredo Vasquez took it with grace, everybody always knew he would have liked the first son named for him. But now, at last, he had a namesake.

Ernesto watched his grandfather go out the door with the baby. Ernesto would have dearly loved to go with them and make it a threesome. But that would have offended his grandmother, so he dismissed the thought.

Though seeing the baby had put Alfredo

Vasquez in a euphoric mood, Eva Vasquez was far less cheerful. She loved her new grandson, of course, but she thought her daughter had enough to cope with. When she learned the fourth child was on the way, she lamented, "Oh, dear, just when the girls are old enough to take care of themselves somewhat, Maria, and you had the chance for a life of your own, perhaps going back to school, maybe even getting the college degree you wanted, starting a career … now … a new baby with all the work that entails."

Ernesto looked longingly out the window to see his grandfather pushing the stroller and singing a silly little Mexican folk song.

"So," Eva Vasquez said, "you've finished your little book on snakes." Maria Sandoval's mother didn't think much of her daughter's new career as a writer of children's books, but at least it was something of a career, though a far cry of what she dreamed of for her bright, only child.

"Lizards, Mom. It's on lizards. Remember the title, *Don't Blink, It's a Skink*," Maria Sandoval said.

"Yes, lizards. Well, I hope it does well. You surely could use the money, with four children now, and Luis earning a modest teacher's salary," Mrs. Vasquez sniffed, sitting down on the couch beside Ernesto. "How is school going, dear?"

"Great. Since I've been senior class president, the principal says the new programs we've put in place are helping a lot of kids. We're tutoring seniors with academic problems, and we have an outreach to at-risk freshmen," Ernesto said.

"That's wonderful, Ernie, just as long as you're not taking on too much and losing ground in your own classes," Mrs. Vasquez said.

"No, no, my GPA has actually gone up," Ernesto said.

Eva Vasquez took an album from her large tote bag. "I don't believe you've seen some of these pictures, Ernie. I thought you might enjoy seeing them."

On the cover of the photo album was a beautiful graduation photo of Maria Sandoval at age seventeen. She was stunning. She looked like a movie star. "Wasn't your mother beautiful when she was your age, Ernie?" his grandmother asked.

"She still is," Ernesto said. Mom smiled.

"Of course she is," Mrs. Vasquez agreed with a tight-lipped smile. "But this was such a special time in her life. She had the whole world at her fingertips. She was senior class president too. Did you know that, Ernie?"

Ernesto nodded. "Mom told me. She gave me a lot of good pointers when I ran for senior class president."

"We were getting ready for your mother to go off to college … look, here are some of the acceptance letters she received from some very prestigious schools. We put them in the album," Eva Vasquez said in a wistful voice. She turned the page to snapshots of a teenaged Maria Sandoval surrounded by posters of the University of California at Los Angeles and the University of California at Berkeley. "We were so excited. She'd be moving into a dorm, and her father and I were anxious to help her fix it up."

Ernesto glanced over at his mother, who was rolling her eyes. Here it was coming again, Grandma's bitter frustration that her only child did not fulfill her potential by going to a fine college and having a career worthy of her talents. Instead she married a poor college student who wanted to be a poorly paid high school teacher, and now she was raising four children and writing about skinks.

"You were going to major in economics, weren't you, dear? You wanted to perhaps run a corporation," Mrs. Vasquez said in an almost anguished voice.

"It was so long ago, Mom." At the time, Luis Sandoval was finishing his student teaching and signing a contract for his first job at a high school in Los Angeles.

Maria Sandoval briefly considered starting college, but soon she was pregnant with Ernesto.

"Look," Mrs. Vasquez continued, turning the pages of the album. "This is what some of her teachers said about your mother, Ernie …"

" 'A brilliant student, destined for a great future.' "

" 'There is nothing this young lady cannot accomplish with her drive and enthusiasm.' "

"Wow, Mom," Ernesto said, "you really had them going."

Mom smiled thinly.

"Sometimes I run into old friends I haven't seen in a long time," Mrs. Vasquez said, "and they can't believe you're not heading a major corporation. Genie Lamont's daughter, you remember her, she wasn't nearly as smart as you, and she's the CEO of a huge public relations firm in New York. Oh, Maria, you gave up so much."

Ernesto wanted to scream. He looked

at his mother's unhappy face and he said, "Grandma, Mom got much more than she gave up. She's got four kids she loves and who love her, and a husband who loves her more than life. That's a lot more than being the CEO of some stupid company."

"Well," Eva Vasquez said, "motherhood is a wonderful thing. I wanted to be a mother too. But I was content with one child, and I was able to have a rewarding career. I think one child is enough for any woman. You can put all your focus on that child and help it develop to its full potential … with a *tribe* of children, you can't meet all their needs, and then there's no life for you either."

"Well, Grandma," Ernesto said, the bitterness growing in his voice. "Maybe you should have had another kid. I mean, then you wouldn't have put all your dreams on Mom. Maybe your other kid would've been a CEO of some investment company on Wall Street. Maybe he or she would have been one of those smart crooks who ripped off all the old people of their life savings."

Mrs. Vasquez stared at Ernesto in shock. "What a terrible thing to say!" she cried.

"I'm just saying, count your blessings, Grandma. Your daughter is the biggest success I ever met. We all love her and our friends love her. When Mom had her last birthday, there were so many people wanted to come, we filled up Hortencia's restaurant. It was a huge party, Grandma, and to see all those happy smiling people who love Mom, you'd think she was a queen or something," Ernesto said.

"It's just that, as a mother, I wanted the best for my child," Eva Vasquez said in a hurt voice. Her words faltered, and she seemed near tears.

Maria Sandoval walked over and sat beside her mother. "Mom, now I *have* the very best, thanks to the wonderful upbringing I got from you and Dad. You should be proud of that. You raised me to stand up for myself and to follow my heart. You raised me to treasure what really matters, and I do." Mom hugged her mother then.

Mrs. Vasquez sighed deeply. "Well, at least you're writing your books. That's something. Writing little books about snakes isn't that impressive, but it's better than spending *all* your time changing diapers," she said.

"Lizards," Ernesto said. "Skinks mainly. Mom's writing about them."

"Where's your husband?" Mrs. Vasquez finally asked.

"Oh, he took Katalina and Juanita down to the ice cream store. They should be back any minute now," Mom said.

"I hope he isn't stuffing those girls with sweets so they get obese," Mrs. Vasquez said. "Obesity is a terrible problem. The children have no faith in the future, and they comfort themselves with junk food."

"Oh, no, Mom," Maria Sandoval said. "The kids love salad, and they eat very few sweets. They sold a lot of tickets at the school raffle, and they won ice cream sundaes. It's a special thing."

"Well, the children have enough against them just living in this neighborhood. On the way in, I noticed so much of that graffiti on the fences and buildings. It was very depressing. Not at all like it used to be. I wish you lived in a nice community like Fred and I do. Speaking of Fred, *where is he*? He's been gone an awfully long time with that baby. Fred is only in his early sixties, but he's not as sharp as he used to be. He might be wandering around lost. He doesn't remember this neighborhood," Mrs. Vasquez said.

"I'm sure Grandpa is fine," Ernesto said. He didn't notice anything wrong with his grandfather's mind.

"The child probably needs changing by now anyway, and he's out there not knowing what to do," Eva Vasquez fretted. "Really, Maria, it was not such a good idea to let him go off with the baby."

"Mom, I tucked a diaper into the stroller just in case," Ernesto's mother said.

"My goodness, Maria, it's been almost

forty years since the man had to deal with a baby who needed changing! What is he going to do with a diaper?" Mrs. Vasquez cried, now thoroughly alarmed.

Just then, the front door opened and Alfredo Vasquez came bounding in, pushing a laughing baby. "Ay, what a time we had. What an adventure. I met all your nice neighbors, Maria. And, Ernesto, I went over to Bluebird Street, and I met your lovely girlfriend! What a darling girl that Naomi is! Oh, and that family! What a riot! Little Alfredo needed a change of wardrobe and Linda, Naomi's mother, she took care of it. Sweet girl, she is. Heckuva bunch of nice people," he said.

Eva Vasquez frowned, "Aren't they that wild bunch you've told me about, Maria?" she asked.

Maria Sandoval looked very guilty. Sometimes she shared too much with her mother, and this was one of those times. "They're okay, Mom," she said hastily. "Just different."

"Oh, that Felix, Naomi's papa. What a gas!" Alfred Vasquez said heartily. "I like that fellow! He wanted to hold Alfredo, and I let him. Oh, Alfredo was chuckling like crazy. Felix said we need to enjoy the little *niño* while he's young because when they grow up, they're not nearly as much fun. Maria, don't you worry about that Martinez family over there. I liked them right away. Alfredo likes them too. He giggled all the time we were there."

Maria Sandoval had frequent misgivings about her son one day marrying Naomi, and the Martinez family being part of the Sandoval family. She had to admit to herself that although she loved Naomi, she wasn't looking forward to Felix Martinez being a part of their family. Even Luis Sandoval sometimes shared those misgivings. But now, Maria was strangely consoled. Her father was a great judge of character, and he instantly bonded with the patriarch of the Martinez clan—Felix Martinez.

Luis Sandoval came home then with

Katalina and Juanita. The girls did not feel as close to Eva Vasquez as they did to *Abuela* Lena, who was part of the family and lived with them. But they ran to their mother's mother and cried, "Hi, *Abuela* Eva!" and then embraced her.

Eva Vasquez frowned and said, "Darlings, we're not Mexicans. We're Americans. We don't use the term *abuela*. I'm your grandma."

The girls embraced their grandfather with more enthusiasm, and the three of them began an animated conversation.

"I took Alfredo to the Martinez house," Mr. Vasquez said, "and we had the time of our lives playing with him."

"Was Felix hollering?" Katalina asked.

"Well, he's a very exuberant man," Mr. Vasquez said. "He's delightful. I like him."

"What's exooberunt?" Juanita asked.

"Full of spirit," Mr. Vasquez said. "Lively."

"Like you, *Abuelo* Alfredo," Katalina said approvingly.

144

Eva Vasquez got up from the sofa and looked at Katalina. "It's *Grandpa* Alfredo, sweetheart."

"And the pit bull," Mr. Vasquez said, "what a great dog."

Eva Vasquez frowned. "I'm getting concerned about your judgment, Fred. Taking a baby in a house with a pit bull!" she scolded.

"It's just old Brutus," Juanita said. "He's like a teddy bear. We play with him all the time."

"Yeah," Katalina said, "he's nicer than most of the boys at school."

"But pit bulls are so dangerous," Eva Vasquez cried.

"He didn't get near little Alfredo," Alfredo Vasquez said, looking perplexed. "He was lying under the table sleeping most of the time. Then, as we were leaving, Felix showed me how he plays ball with Brutus, and I was holding little Alfredo in my arms and he laughed and laughed."

Luis Sandoval was leaning against the

frame of the door. Ernesto met his father's gaze, and their looks expressed a fervent wish: *Make her leave. Make her go away. Soon.*

Dinner passed with strained pleasantries. Maria Sandoval showed her mother some of the artwork for her skink book. Eva Vasquez looked bored. Finally it was over and the Vasquezes drove away. The Sandovals waved from the front yard until the car disappeared onto Tremayne Street.

The four of them stood there in the driveway, all of them thinking the same thing, but nobody wanting to say it. At last Maria Sandoval said, "If only Dad could come alone once in a while. Mom's been talking about taking a cruise to Alaska with some of her friends. Dad isn't interested. Wouldn't it be great if while she was gone, he came down by himself and stayed with us."

"That'd be nice," Ernesto said. "Little Alfredo and his grandfather could really bond."

"It'd be fun," Juanita said. "I'd like to take walks with *Abuelo* Alfredo. He makes me laugh."

"Me too," Katalina said. "I'd like to go places with him … like to the zoo."

"I love my mother," Maria Sandoval said in a measured voice, "but she'll never get over her disappointment that I didn't go on to college and have a career. When I was growing up, Mom always told me to follow my heart when I made decisions, but then when I did that, she was so furious and sad."

Luis Sandoval put his arms around his wife and kissed her. "How lucky I am, *querida mia*, that you followed your heart. I cannot imagine my life without you."

"Oh, Luis," Ernesto's mother said. "Mom was so indignant about something Ernesto said. Just before she put on her coat to leave, when nobody was around to hear her except me, she said she thinks our son is picking up bad manners from his friends in the *barrio*."

"Yeah," Ernesto said. He was close enough now to hear what his mother was saying to his father. "She was going on and on about how terrible it is that her only child, Mom, doesn't have some big career ... so I told her she shoulda had another kid."

Mom got a wry look. "Ernie, you said maybe her other child would have made it to Wall Street and been one of those people cheating the old people out of their money. I guess that was kinda rude, Ernie, don't you think?"

"Yeah, I guess so," Ernesto said.

Luis Sandoval covered his mouth to suppress a grin.

"Anyway," Ernesto said, "Grandpa had a fabulous time. I've never seen him so joyful. He really loves his little namesake. I think little Alfredo is going to make Grandpa happier than anything else in the world."

Ernesto was heading for his room to check any messages he got when his phone rang.

"Yeah? What's up?" he said.

"Ernie," Mira Nuñez said. "I hate so much to bother you all the time. You were so nice in helping me before, but now something awful has happened."

"Oh no," Ernesto said under his breath, rolling his eyes. He thought to himself, "How did I get involved with this chick? *Why me*?" To Mira, Ernesto said, "What's wrong now?"

"You wouldn't believe what some evil person did. They called Clay up and said I'd been over to Kenny Trujillo's house last night. I swore to Clay it was a lie just to cause trouble between us, but he's all upset. Ernie, do you think Paul Morales and his friends would do a thing like that?" Mira asked.

"Absolutely not," Ernesto said. He felt sick. He didn't want any part of this. "Mira, my friends promised me they'd keep out of your business with Clay. So what's going on—didn't Clay believe you?"

Mira began to cry.

CHAPTER NINE

Oh, Ernie," Mira said, "it's not that Clay is being mean to me or anything … I mean, his reaction was almost worse than what he usually does, get mad and start yelling. He just looked devastated. I mean, he looked heartbroken, Ernie. It just broke my heart to see him so hurt."

"Did Clay recognize the voice on the phone?" Ernesto asked.

"Clay said it sounded like a kid. Somebody younger than us. Clay thought it might be a middle schooler or maybe somebody in ninth grade," Mira said.

"So, some little twit is just making a joke," Ernesto said impatiently. "Some boneheaded little jerk is having a laugh.

What has Clay done lately to get a young kid mad at him? The guy has a gift for annoying people. Did he maybe cuss out a skateboarder from his car or something?"

"But, Ernie, the kid had to know about me and Kenny and Clay. It has to be somebody who knows us all well enough to know that making a call like that is like throwing gasoline on a fire … how can people be so mean, Ernie? I've never been happier in my entire life, and Clay is on top of the world too. Who'd be cruel enough to want to bring us down?" Mira wept.

"I'll see what I can find out, Mira," Ernesto said. "In the meantime, tell Clay to chill out. Even somebody with a pea brain has got to see through this as a prank."

When Ernesto ended the call, his mother said, "What's that all about?"

"Oh, Mira Nuñez. This dumb chick is back with Clay Aguirre, and now somebody is trying to split them up by saying that Mira is back with her other old boyfriend, Kenny Trujillo," Ernesto said.

"Oh, Mrs. Trujillo told me about how bad Kenny feels," Maria Sandoval said.

Ernesto checked out Clay Aguirre's Facebook page. There were pictures of Clay playing football and photos with him and Mira. There were a lot of messages posted congratulating Clay on his football victory. There were a few uncivil messages from Lincoln players warning Clay he'd never get to the regional championships with the Cougars. And then one post caught Ernesto's attention.

"Hey, Aguirre, you're not man enough for a chick like Mira Nuñez. A better dude is gonna take her away from you right under your nose. Ha-ha."

Maria Sandoval read the message over Ernesto's shoulder. "Could be somebody from Lincoln just trying to hurt Clay," she said. "Why don't you just tell Mira to ignore it? Clay should do the same."

"I kinda feel sorry for Mira. Her mom is out dating twenty-four-seven, and she hasn't got any real home life," Ernesto said.

"You're so big-hearted, Ernie, but don't let it drag you down," Mom said. "You can't fix the world."

Ernesto recalled that Clay Aguirre had gotten so angry at Naomi Martinez last year when he thought she was showing interest in Ernesto that he slapped her hard across the face and left a serious bruise. Ernesto wondered if that's where it was going with Clay and Mira. If Clay really believed he was losing her, would he get violent? He had done it before. Ernesto wasn't sure that Mira was right in insisting that Clay had changed for the better. Maybe he had and maybe not.

Maybe, Ernesto thought, somebody out there was trying to push Clay Aguirre's buttons so he would unleash his rage against Mira and show her what he was really like. It was a dangerous game for somebody to be playing. It was putting Mira Nuñez at risk. When a guy like Clay flew into a jealous rage, he might do even more damage to the girl than he did to Naomi.

153

Ernesto thought of him then—of Kenny Trujillo. Kenny had mentioned doing something to make Clay revert to his old self. He thought that would open Mira's eyes once and for all. Ernesto had warned him that that was playing with fire, but maybe Kenny was so desperate to get Mira back that he was willing to take the chance that she'd be hurt in the process.

Ernesto turned ice cold. He never liked Clay Aguirre. When Clay left Naomi's face all bruised that time, Ernesto hated him, pure and simple. Ernesto could never feel good about a guy who'd hurt a girl like that.

But in a way, if Kenny Trujillo was behind this campaign to make Clay angry enough to explode against Mira, he was just as evil as Clay.

What if Kenny had hired some kid to make that call to Clay? What if Kenny had posted that message on Clay's Facebook wall?

At school the next day, Ernesto looked

154

for Kenny Trujillo. When he saw him walking onto campus, he approached him. "Kenny, I need a word with you," he said.

Kenny stuck out his hands in his pockets and said, "Okay."

"Kenny, somebody is trying to yank Clay Aguirre's chain by making phone calls to him that Mira Nuñez is seeing you on the sly. Remember when we talked the other day? You said you'd like to force Clay into showing Mira his true colors," Ernesto said.

"And you think I'm doing that stuff?" Kenny asked.

"I didn't say that, man," Ernesto said. "But it sorta clicked in my brain what you'd said, and if it was you, then I thought—"

"I don't know anything about it," Kenny snapped.

"Kenny, I know that you care about Mira and it's got me worried that someone would just try to stir Aguirre into a rage where he might hurt Mira … that's what's got me worried," Ernesto said.

A hard look came to Kenny's face.

"Why's she hanging with a dude who's a ticking time bomb? He's gonna hurt her sooner or later anyway. That kind always does. She's like walking on eggshells with him. I didn't make no phone call, but maybe whoever did is doing the chick a favor. If she breaks up with Aguirre now, maybe she'll be lucky and get nothing but a black eye. If she hangs with him over the long haul, who knows what he might do to her if he has reason to be jealous. You hear about stuff like that all the time. Girls end up hurt bad or dead," he said.

"Okay, if you say you're not doing it, Kenny, that's good enough for me. But whoever is doing it isn't doing Mira any favors, dude," Ernesto said. He wasn't sure if he believed Kenny Trujillo's denial or not. He was leaning toward not believing it.

At lunchtime, Ernesto saw Clay and Mira walking to their favorite lunch spot behind the library. They never brought lunches. They always bought something in the machines. Ernesto couldn't understand that. He thought the sandwiches in the machines were barely edible.

Ernesto looked closely at the pair. They seemed to be getting along. Clay was laughing about something and Mira was smiling too. Maybe, Ernesto thought hopefully, Clay *had* changed. It wasn't impossible. People could redeem themselves. And maybe Clay *did* have a few grains of decency. After all, when he spotted that little freshman, Bobby Padilla, hiding at the warehouse, he did come and tell Ernesto so they could rescue the boy. Clay didn't have to do that.

Sure, Clay Aguirre had slapped Naomi so hard he left bruises last year. But maybe that was a traumatic moment for him as well as for her. Maybe deep inside he had loved Naomi very much and a part of him would always grieve for the girl he'd lost in a moment of rage. Maybe during that violent moment, Naomi lost her trust in Clay, but also Clay learned the terrible price of violence.

Ernesto hoped that was the way it was, for Mira's sake.

Ernesto had lunch with Julio Avila and their other friends in the usual place. Abel had once more generously packed sandwiches for everybody, but they all kicked in for the fixings.

"We gotta do something spectacular for this guy," Ernesto said, "when he makes gourmet lunches like this."

"Ahhh," Abel said. "It's fun. I love to see your face light up when you bite into salsa chicken instead of your peanut butter and jelly sandwich, Ernie."

Naomi looked at Ernesto and said, "Your grandfather came to our house Sunday. He's just too adorable for words. I've met him before briefly, Ernie, but seeing him and the baby interacting, it was just precious."

Ernesto laughed. "He loved you guys. Your dad really impressed him. They're both football fanatics, and they have the same political ideas. Usually when people first meet your dad, they're a little intimidated, but not my grandpa," Ernesto said.

"I know," Naomi said. "They became lifelong buddies in five minutes. I was so happy. I thought my dad would tick your grandpa off about something, but they even both love pit bulls."

Penelope Ruiz came walking over in the middle of the lunch period. "Hi, everybody. I got a scoop," the ninth-grade sister of Abel Ruiz said.

"Yeah," Abel said, "what's up, squirt?"

"You know that little cockroach Rocky Salcedo, the one always mocking me and calling me fat?" Penelope said. "Well, he's flashing a ten dollar bill. He said he got it from some senior for making a phone call to mess up some dude and his girlfriend."

Ernesto stiffened. Clay had told Mira the voice on the phone sounded like a younger kid. "He give any names, Penny?" he asked.

"No way," Penelope said. "He's hoping the dude asks him to make another call so he can score another ten. He is such a little weasel. He'd sell out his grandmother if the price was right."

After school, Ernesto walked over to the freshman parking lot where the parents waited for their ninth graders who didn't take the bus or walk home. He spotted Rocky Salcedo heading for the bus stop. His parents weren't getting him today.

"Hey, Rocky," Ernesto said, "I got something to say to you."

Rocky glared at Ernesto. He blamed Ernesto for helping get him in trouble for bullying the other freshmen. "Get lost, fool," Rocky hissed at the tall senior.

"Then you don't want this," Ernesto said, pulling out a ten dollar bill.

Rocky's eyes widened. He reminded Ernesto of a snake sizing up a mouse for lunch. "What for?" he asked.

"I want to know the name of the dude who paid you to call Clay Aguirre," Ernesto said.

Rocky looked flustered. He didn't know

whether to admit what he'd done and give Ernesto what he wanted for the ten, or if he should deny everything. He was scared of Ernesto, afraid that what he'd done was going to get him in trouble. "I never called nobody," he muttered.

"Rocky, somebody heard you make the call. You're busted if you don't help me here," Ernesto said, though he was faking it. Nobody heard Rocky make the call except the guy who paid him to make the call.

Rocky was now more scared. "You still give me the ten if I tell you who it was?" he asked warily.

"It's a deal," Ernesto said.

"I don't know the dude's name," Rocky said. "But he always wears a striped green hoodie."

Ernesto gave Rocky the ten. But he said, "Don't ever do anything like that again, Rocky." Ernesto grabbed Rocky's sweatshirt and pulled him close to his face. "Listen up, you do something like that again, you're in so much hot water you'll think you're a lobster, dude. Understand?" Ernesto gave him a little shake.

When Ernesto let go of the boy's sweat-shirt, he ran like a deer for the bus stop, never looking back.

Ernesto felt really sad. Kenny Trujillo always wore a striped green hoodie. Ernesto never thought Kenny was a bad guy, and it shook him to realize he'd done such a bad thing. Ernesto wasn't sure what to do now that he knew, but he had to do something. He couldn't tell Mira or Clay what Kenny had done. He couldn't rat the guy out and risk Clay maybe pulverizing him.

Kenny Trujillo lived in an apartment with his mother on Cardinal Street. Kenny had told Ernesto that his own father was a man much like Clay, nice when everything was going his way, a bear when it wasn't. The father and mother were long divorced, but Mira had learned an ugly pattern from her mother. Mrs. Trujillo had spent most of her married life desperately trying to avoid making her husband mad for fear of the consequences. Now Mira was determined to spare Clay from anything upsetting for fear of his nasty reaction.

Kenny seemed surprised when Ernesto appeared at his door. His mother had left for work already, and he was alone.

"May I come in, man?" Ernesto asked.

Kenny stepped back. "Sure. What's going on?" He seemed nervous. Maybe he saw in Ernesto's face that he had figured things out.

They went into a plain but neat living room. Mrs. Trujillo earned a modest salary as a nurse's aide in a rest home. On the wall were pictures of Kenny from first grade on. He was his mother's only child, and she was proud of him. There were no pictures of the father.

"Kenny, you told me you weren't hassling Aguirre," Ernesto said in a soft voice, "but you are. You hired a ninth grader to make that call."

"That's a lie," Kenny said in a desperate voice. His eyes were filled with fear. "I didn't do anything. I just talked to Mira and told her how much I missed her."

"Dude, I didn't tell anybody, and I won't," Ernesto said. "I won't tell Mira or Clay. Clay can be a bad enemy, and I don't want to get anybody hurt. You hear where I'm coming from? Thing is, I was glad when you and Mira were together. It made me sick when she went back to Clay. But she has the right to do what she wants. She has the right to be stupid, okay?"

Kenny Trujillo sat in the chair, hanging his head. He clasped and unclasped his hands. "Okay, I did it. I didn't do it just for myself. I did it for her. He's no good for her. He's no good for any chick." Kenny looked up at Ernesto.

"You don't get it, Ernie. For most of my life I've lived with a guy like Clay Aguirre— my father. We were always scared, Mom and me. Would this make him mad? How about that? Should we hide the utility bill until he's in a better mood? I watched my mother struggling with a mean man, never knowing when the bombs would start falling. He never hurt mom bad. He pushed her and one time sorta choked her. But mostly he called her names, bad, ugly names."

Kenny swallowed, his face pale. "When she finally got the courage to divorce him, it was terrible for a little while. He couldn't believe what was happening. She had to get a restraining order. I was afraid I'd come home from school and find her on the floor … but, it worked. He left. It's so great now to come home from school and know there won't be fighting and yelling and dirty words, wondering what mood my father will be in. I just didn't want that for Mira, Ernie. I just thought there had to be a way to wake her up before it was too late."

"Kenny, I hear you," Ernesto said. "I'm even saying maybe you're right to have done what you did, but you gotta stop now. You go and talk to Mira if you want to. Tell her what you and your mom went through with your dad. Try to win her back, Kenny, but do it in a straight-up way. It's not fair to do it like you've been doing, and it's dangerous. If you push Clay too far and he ends up hurting Mira, then you got blood on your hands, man."

"I have talked to her … she won't listen," Kenny said.

Ernesto nodded. "I've talked to her too. Most of her friends have," he said. "Kenny, maybe Clay Aguirre will get mad about something and blow up so bad that Mira will see him for what he is … if that happens, maybe she'll fall out of love with him like she did before, and you got a chance to catch her when she falls. But you can't be the one making it happen. There's something evil about pushing somebody into becoming some kind of a monster just to prove that he *is* a monster."

"And if I don't back off, then you'll blow my cover, right?" Kenny said in a bitter voice. "You'll tell them, Mira and Aguirre, what I did … and she'll end up hating me."

"No, I won't ever do that," Ernesto said. "I swear to you, Kenny, that I won't ever do that. I'm here to ask you to do the right thing, but it's up to you. I think you're a great guy, Kenny. I don't think you want to hurt anybody. But what you're doing is just wrong. You got a conscience, dude, and I know it's telling you what you're doing is wrong." Ernesto got up. "That's all I've got to say."

Ernesto felt bad about what he'd just done, but he had no choice. If Kenny continued harassing Clay Aguirre with lies, Ernesto wouldn't tell on him. He meant that. But Ernesto had a strong feeling that he had convinced Kenny Trujillo to back off. The guy had enough decency for that.

Ernesto left the apartment and went down to his Volvo. He sat in the car for a few minutes, his eyes closed. Then he started the car up and went home.

When Ernesto was in his room studying that night, Mira called. The minute he heard her voice, he stiffened. It had happened. Again, he thought. Kenny was not going to quit. Ernesto had misjudged him.

"Hi, Mira," Ernesto said wearily. "So …"

"Did you find out anything about who called Clay, Ernie?" Mira asked.

"No. Probably just some stupid little punk wanting trouble," Ernesto said.

"Ernie, you know what Clay told me tonight? He told me he believed me. He said he trusted me. He said he was sorry for the times he made me sad. I cried, Ernie. I … I think it's gonna be okay now. I really think so."

CHAPTER TEN

During lunch at Cesar Chavez High on Wednesday, Naomi Martinez said, "Ernie, you want to go see the Cougars play Friday night at Taft? It's gonna be a really big game. Taft is awesome."

"Oh yes," Ernesto said. "Watch my dear buddy Clay Aguirre win more gridiron glory." A wry look turned Ernesto's lips. "But I gotta go, babe. I don't want all the Chavez jocks to think I don't love football as much as they do. I *am* senior class president, and what kind of a jerk would I be if I didn't sit there rooting for the Cougars to move on in the championship games?"

Naomi giggled. "Rah, rah, rah," she said.

"Yeah, I want to make sure everybody knows I think who wins the divisional championship is every bit as important as the world agreeing on a treaty to ban all nuclear weapons and spare the planet from annihilation," Ernesto said.

"Clay has been going around on cloud nine since he made that big play in the game against Lincoln," Naomi said. "But I think Taft will be tougher."

Ernesto was relieved that Kenny Trujillo had apparently stopped his harassment campaign to break up Clay and Mira. Ernesto did not share the details of that with anybody, not even Naomi. One of the rules Ernesto lived by was to protect the reputation of other people. He didn't want to spread the word that Kenny had paid a ninth grader to call Clay and tell him that Mira was cheating on him, which was a lie. Luis Sandoval held to those same principles. He taught them to his son. Mr. Sandoval never shared personal information about his students with other teachers. He really respected the privacy of his students.

"There's always a chance that the Cougars will come up short," Ernesto said. "I really hope we win, but Taft has a killer quarterback and the defense is awesome. I remember when Clay was a junior, and he was always getting tackled. It could happen Friday."

"Yeah, you never know," Naomi said.

"Of course, the bad Ernesto Sandoval would like to see Clay knocked off his high horse, but the good Ernesto just wants the best team to win, and that has to be us," Ernesto said. "I've disliked Clay for a long time, but lately I'm seeing tiny sparks of character. Maybe a miracle is happening."

Naomi leaned over and kissed Ernesto on the cheek. She'd been eating a ham sandwich with lots of mustard, and now Ernesto had mustard all over his cheek, but he didn't mind. No price was too heavy to pay for a kiss from Naomi.

"You know, Ernie, that's one of the

things that makes you so lovable. With all the bad blood between you and Clay, you're willing to give him the benefit of the doubt that he might be changing. I could never love somebody who held on to grudges."

There were a lot of cars from Cesar Chavez High School parked at Taft for the game in addition to the buses that transported the team and some fans. Both schools had warned their fans about causing trouble when the game was over. In the past there had been fist fights and slashed tires after some hotly contested games. Ernesto had warned the seniors that nobody from Chavez should disgrace their school in that way.

When the Cougars marched out onto the playing field under the brilliant lights of the football turf, Clay Aguirre seemed to have grown a few more inches. Of course, he hadn't, but his proud stance made it look that way. He looked like Superman with his bulging muscles. Mira glanced at Clay, a look of pure joy on her face.

Clay Aguirre had made a lot of enemies

at Chavez because, to be honest, he wasn't often a nice guy. But as long as he was playing a role in the Cougar wins, all was forgiven. But, Ernesto figured, if he blew it, then he'd be back to being a goat.

In the first few minutes of the game, the Chavez fans suffered a major panic attack. The Taft Tigers put seven points on the board when their quarterback, an amazing kid that reminded everybody of Cam Newton, marched into the end zone for a touchdown.

Mira Nuñez looked distraught.

Donny Miranda, quarterbacking for the Cougars, evened the score with a thirteen-yard touchdown pass. Clay Aguirre was tackled, and he began to look like he wasn't going to be the star tonight. In fact, he was limping after the hard hit.

Miranda threw another touchdown pass in the third quarter, and the score went to fourteen to seven. The Chavez fans were on their feet. It looked like it was going to be a good night, and Chavez would continue to be in the hunt.

Donny Miranda changed all that. He fumbled the ball in the fourth quarter and the Tiger QB, Kawli Fisher, turned the fumble into a touchdown for Taft.

The score was tied fourteen–fourteen when Kawli got hot and scored two more TDs. The Taft fans went crazy, and a pall settled over the Chavez cheering section.

"I just want to get out of here," Ernesto said after the game. He grabbed Naomi's hand and they made for the parking lot. The final score was twenty-eight Taft and fourteen Chavez. Taft was going on, and Chavez was going home.

The Chavez team was planning a big celebration at Hortencia's if they won, but none of that happened now.

"I feel sorry for Mira," Naomi said as they drove from the parking lot. "I remember when I was dating Clay and he made a poor showing, he was impossible. I just dreaded those times. He'd rant and rave and blame everybody but himself."

"Well, tonight will be a real test for their

relationship. If Clay can keep his cool, then maybe they got a chance. If not, maybe this is the night Mira bails," Ernesto said. He turned to Naomi and said, "It's early yet. I got an idea, but I'm not sure you'd want to go along."

"Let's hear it, Ernie," Naomi said.

"Today is Richie Loranzo's birthday. I asked him if he was doing anything special, and he said his foster parents were having a little party, cake and stuff, just them and a couple friends of Richie's, Angel and Bobby." All three of the freshmen were in Ernesto's mentoring program for at-risk kids. "I sort of overheard Richie saying he'd like some decent athletic shoes for playing basketball. He wears those run-down deals. I got him a gift certificate for that cool sports store in the mall so he can go pick out what he likes. I was going to give it to him at school on Monday, but maybe we could crash the party. It's probably ending, and I could slip him my gift. It would be like the cherry on the top of a sundae. You think?"

"Oh, Ernie, that sounds wonderful! Let's do it!" Naomi said. "I bet he'll be thrilled."

Ernesto grinned. "I kinda thought you'd like that idea, babe," he said.

They drove to Starling Street and pulled into the driveway of the Bejarañas, Richie's foster parents.

"Hey, it looks dark," Ernesto said. "The party must have broken up really early." There was disappointment in Ernesto's voice.

"There's some kind of light in the front room," Naomi said. "Somebody's home."

They got out of the Volvo and rang the front doorbell. Richie Loranzo opened up. They could see the television screen flickering in the living room. He'd been watching TV.

"Hey, Richie," Ernesto said, "the birthday party shut down early, huh?"

"No party," Richie said, shrugging his shoulders. He was struggling to be cool. "I called the kids, Angel and Bobby, and told them not to come. Sam and Arlene got a call from their daughter. She's moving to a new apartment, and she wanted them to come help her move. They told me they'd have a birthday party for me some other time. No big deal. I don't care. It's kid stuff anyway."

Sam and Arlene Bejaraña were good foster parents. They made sure Richie had what he needed. And you couldn't expect them to put a foster kid's birthday party ahead of their own daughter's request for help in moving. Richie was not their kid. He was nobody's kid now.

"So you're all alone, huh, Richie?" Ernesto asked.

"Yeah, it's okay," Richie said. "I'm watching TV." Richie always looked sad, but right now he looked sadder than usual.

"So when are Sam and Arlene coming home?" Ernesto asked.

"They said maybe one or two in the morning. Their daughter lives up in Orange County," Richie said. "They asked me if I'd be okay here by myself, and I said sure. I'm fifteen years old now."

"Richie, me and Naomi just came from a big football game. Chavez lost. It was a major bummer, and we're feeling crummy. You want to help cheer us up and get something to eat at the Plaza? They're serving super cheeseburgers and chocolate shakes."

Richie hesitated. "You guys aren't just trying to, you know, make it up to me or something, 'cause it's no big deal," he said. But his eyes flickered with hope.

"No way," Naomi spoke up. "We had nothing to eat at the football game but stale popcorn, and we're starved."

"Well, okay, then," Richie said, hurrying to get his jacket.

"Leave a note for Sam and Arlene in case they get home early," Ernesto said. Richie scribbled a note and the three of them went out the door.

"You like hamburgers, huh, Richie?" Ernesto said as they drove toward the Plaza.

"Yeah, I *love* 'em," Richie said.

"Well, these here at the Plaza aren't your regular burgers," Ernesto said. "They are so juicy and yummy."

When they parked at the hamburger joint and went in, Ernesto tipped off the waiter that the boy was having a birthday and asked if the staff could do something special at the end of the meal.

"Wow," Richie said when he began eating the burger. "This is awesome. It's got onion rings and mushrooms and no tiny dried up pickle, but big pickle slices. And the sauce. Wow!"

Ernesto grinned. "Yeah, they know how to do it right here." Ernesto was keeping up the heavy chatter with the boy, but deep in his heart he ached to think of what it must have been like for Richie when the birthday party was canceled. Richie had told everyone at school he was having a party with cake and punch and a couple balloons. He invited Angel Roma and Bobby Padilla, and then to have it all canceled. He must have felt humiliated to have to call Angel and Bobby and tell them not to come, that something more important had come up and his foster parents weren't having a party for him after all.

Ernesto thought to himself that helping the daughter move had to have been awfully important for them to break this kid's heart when it had been broken so much already. To think of Richie sitting alone in that dark house watching TV made Ernesto sick. On his fifteenth birthday. It had to be total confirmation that nobody cared about him.

When they had finished their hamburgers, a trio of waitresses appeared at their table, singing joyfully, "Happy birthday, Richie. All our best to you. You're a handsome young man. And an awesome one too."

Richie flushed pink, but he was still smiling when they set a huge slice of cake with a candle in the middle at his place. "Hey," Richie said, "this is pretty cool. Wait'll I tell Bobby and Angel what happened!"

As they ate their dessert, Ernesto

asked, "So you want to play basketball, eh, Richie?"

"Yeah, I love basketball. Coach said I'm pretty good too. I'm getting really tall. Being tall runs in my family … my father," his voice trailed off. He swallowed and said, "My father played basketball in high school. I love the Lakers. Those guys are so amazing. But I like playing better than watching. Coach says he thinks I'm good enough to be on the Cougar team."

"Chavez High has always had a strong basketball team," Naomi said. "I love watching it."

"Yeah, you know," Richie said, "my grandparents, they don't live around here. They live in Florida, but they sent me some money for my birthday. They sent me fifteen dollars, and I'm saving it so I can get some good athletic shoes for playing basketball. I make a little money doing odd jobs around the neighborhood, and pretty soon I'll have enough money for the shoes. I want shoes like the pros wear."

Naomi looked at Ernesto. He reached into his pocket and pulled out an envelope. He had bought a birthday card for Richie. It was designed for a teenage boy who liked basketball. It showed a tall, gangly cartoonish looking kid wearing oversized shoes, making a jump shot.

The message on the inside of the card was "You'll go far. You're already a star!"

Ernesto had written, "Happy birthday to Richie, a cool dude."

Richie's eyes got very big. "Wow, you got me a birthday card, Ernie?" He laughed when he saw the kid on the card.

"Sure," Ernesto said, "you're my bro, Richie. That's not just a sometime thing. I got a stake in you. I got another little brother at home, Alfredo, but he's only a baby, and he's not as much fun yet as you are, Richie."

Richie saw the gift certificate then. His eyes got even bigger. It was for the sports store where he hoped to get his athletic shoes when he had saved enough money.

Richie's eyes widened into saucers, filling his thin face. "No way, no way," he kept saying.

"Way," Ernesto laughed. "You can pay me back by helping the Cougars win a bunch of games. You're just a freshman, Richie. You got three more years here at Chavez, and by the time you're a senior, you'll be so great the Lakers will probably be hearing about you."

Richie didn't cry, but his big eyes looked damp. "Aw, Ernie," he said in a hoarse voice. "I never thought you'd do anything like this. Gosh, Ernie, thanks."

Ernesto and Naomi took Richie home well before midnight. The foster parents weren't home yet. But there was a message on the phone.

Richie said, "Sam wants to know if I'm doing okay."

"Call him, Richie," Ernesto said.

Richie called Sam Bejaraña on his cell. From what Richie was saying, Ernesto could tell the man was apologizing for how the evening turned out. He was having some guilt over disappointing the boy.

"It's okay, Sam," Richie said, his voice throbbing with excitement. "I got a big surprise. My mentor from school and his girlfriend, they came to see me. I had the best birthday I ever had in my whole life. We went to the Plaza and had these amazing burgers, and they sang a happy birthday song to me and we had cake … and there was even a candle in the cake," Richie's voice was rushing. "And, and Ernie, … he just gave me a gift certificate for those shoes I been needing. I can get them this weekend, and then I can join the team at school … yeah! Sure, it's okay. It's no big deal. Tonight was better than any old party, Sam. It was way better."

Before Ernesto and Naomi left, Ernesto extended his hand and said, "Happy birthday, Richie. See you at school Monday."

Richie looked at the tall senior. Richie knew he was now fifteen years old and too old for mush stuff, but he didn't care. He ignored Ernesto's hand and threw his arms around Ernesto, and in a voice muffled by emotion said, "Thanks, Ernie … you're the … best."

Ernesto hugged Richie Loranzo and then Naomi hugged him. Before they left, they made sure all the doors were securely locked, and then they went to the Volvo to head home.

"He'll never forget tonight, Ernie," Naomi said.

"Neither will I," Ernesto said. "To think we might not even have stopped over … that he would have had nothing but watching TV on his birthday."

Naomi squeezed Ernesto's hand. "The kid is right," she said.

"What?" Ernesto said.

"You *are* the best, Ernie," Naomi said.

Ernesto gave Naomi a long kiss before dropping her at the Martinez house. They clung to each other as long as they could.

Then Ernesto waited until Naomi was safely inside before going home himself.

At Cesar Chavez High School on Monday, there were some long faces. They were still sad about being knocked out of the running for the divisional football championship.

As Naomi and Ernesto walked toward their first classes, they spotted Clay Aguirre getting out of his car. His shoulders were slumping visibly. He had not been able to help the Cougars on Friday night.

"Hey, Aguirre," a junior yelled. "You were lame on the field, dude."

"Oh man, here we go," Ernesto said.

Mira Nuñez heard the taunt, and she looked stricken. Clay Aguirre stood there for a moment; then he straightened his shoulders and walked toward Mira.

"Babe," Mira said in an almost tearful voice, "I'm so sorry."

A very faint smile came across Clay Aguirre's face. It could not quite cover the hurt in his eyes, but it helped. "It's okay, babe," he said, reaching for the girl's hand and pulling her into his arms.

Ernesto remembered what Mira Nuñez had said to him once. She asked him if he didn't think people could change. Ernesto gave her a reluctant " 'I guess so.' "

Ernesto now thought maybe such a thing had happened. And then Clay Aguirre spotted Ernesto staring at him. "You got something to say, Sandoval? You wanna gloat about the game?"

"No way, Aguirre," Ernesto said. "I'm just on my way to the vending machine for a pear."

After he got his pear, Ernesto had a few minutes to reflect before class. He didn't like the way he'd reacted to Rod Garcia's taunting. And he now knew his temper could get the better of him. The best person he could be, he thought, was the person who was there for his friends. He liked *that* Ernesto.

He liked helping people. He'd helped

Mira and Clay; even though Clay didn't deserve it, Mira sure did. He'd helped Kenny Trujillo move on, or at least he hoped he did. And he felt great about helping Richie Loranzo. "I'll be there for them," he said to himself. "I'll be there."